RED

READ ALL OF LIESL SHURTLIFF'S (FAIRLY) TRUE TALES

———◆◆◆———

RED

THE (FAIRLY) TRUE TALE OF
RED RIDING HOOD

LIESL SHURTLIFF

A YEARLING BOOK

Text copyright © 2016 by Liesl Shurtliff
Cover art copyright © 2018 by Kevin Keele
Title type copyright © 2018 by Jacey

All rights reserved. Published in the United States by Yearling, an imprint of Random House Children's Books, a division of Penguin Random House LLC, New York. Originally published under the title *Red: The True Story of Red Riding Hood* in hardcover in the United States by Alfred A. Knopf, an imprint of Random House Children's Books, New York, in 2016.

Yearling and the jumping horse design are registered trademarks of Penguin Random House LLC.

Visit us on the Web! rhcbooks.com
Educators and librarians, for a variety of teaching tools, visit us at RHTeachersLibrarians.com

The Library of Congress has cataloged the hardcover edition of this work as follows:
Shurtliff, Liesl.
Title: Red : the true story of Red Riding Hood / Liesl Shurtliff.
Description: First edition. | New York : Alfred A. Knopf, [2016] | Summary: "Followed by a wolf, a huntsman, and a porridge-sampling nuisance called Goldie, Red embarks on a quest to find a magical cure for her ailing grandmother." —Provided by publisher
Identifiers: LCCN 2015022144 | ISBN 978-0-385-75583-2 (trade) |
ISBN 978-0-385-75584-9 (lib. bdg.) | ISBN 978-0-385-75585-6 (ebook)
Subjects: | CYAC: Fairy tales. | Adventure and adventurers—Fiction. | Characters in literature—Fiction. | Witches—Fiction. | Wolves—Fiction. | Grandmothers—Fiction. | BISAC: JUVENILE FICTION / Fairy Tales & Folklore / Adaptations.
Classification: LCC PZ8.S34525 Red 2016 | DDC [Fic]—dc23
ISBN 978-0-385-75586-3 (pbk.)

Printed in the United States of America
10 9 8 7 6

In loving memory of my grandmother
Ann Cardall Robbins Bunting,
who was *gorgeous*. And hilarious.
I miss you.

CONTENTS

CHAPTER ONE
Magical Mistakes

The first time I tried my hand at magic, I grew roses out of my nose. This was not my intention. I meant to grow flowers out of the *ground*, like any normal person would. But I've never been normal, and magic is unpredictable, finicky, and dangerous, especially in the wrong hands.

Granny had taught me magic from the cradle. Some grandmothers shower their grandbabies with cuddles and kisses and gumdrops. I got enchantments and spells and potions. Granny knew spells to conjure rain and wind, charms to make things grow or shrink, and enchantments of disguise and trickery. She could brew a potion to clear your mind or clear your stuffy nose. She had elixirs for toothaches, bellyaches, and heartaches, and a special balm for bottom itch. There was no end to the wonders of magic.

There was also no end to the troubles.

When I was five years old, I wanted to grow red roses for Granny's birthday. Roses, because her name is Rose, and red, because my name is Red. They would be the perfect gift. I knew I could do it. I had seen Granny grow fat orange pumpkins and juicy red berries straight out of the ground with just a wave of her hands and a few words.

I chose my own words with care.

Red Rose Charm
Sprout and blossom, red, red rose
Let your fragrance fill my nose

I felt the tingle of the magic in my fingertips. I gave a flourish of the arm, a flick of the hand, just as Granny did, but nothing happened. I tried again. I spoke louder, flourished grander, and . . .

A red rose exploded out of my right nostril.

I tried to rub the rose off, but that only made me sneeze, and another rose shot out of my left nostril.

Granny could not stop laughing. You might even say she cackled.

"Granny! Do some-ding!" I sobbed through the roses. I expected her to wave her hands and make the roses disappear. Instead, she ripped them right out of my nose.

"Aaaaouch!" I screamed.

"Thank you for the roses," said Granny, placing them in a vase on her table. "We can call them booger blossoms."

"*Achoo!*" I replied.

Granny laughed for a full five minutes.

I sneezed for five hours.

I'll admit, it was sort of funny, even if it did hurt worse than pixie bites. But I worried that this might be an omen—that the magic was somehow wrong inside me.

After the booger blossoms, I decided to stick to practical magic, such as a drying spell. I'd seen Granny do this countless times: just a snap of her fingers and she'd have dripping laundry dry in minutes.

But when I snapped my fingers, no wind came. Just fire. Yes, *fire*, as in flames. Flaming skirts and blouses and undergarments. In less than a minute, they were cinders and ash.

"Well, they're certainly dry," said Granny.

When I was six, I had a friend named Gertie. We were only allowed to play at her house with constant supervision from her mother, Helga. Helga was always worried. She worried Gertie would fall in a well or off a cliff. She worried Gertie would choke on her morning mush. She worried trolls would come in the night and carry Gertie away for their supper. This worrying became problematic when I wanted to take Gertie into The Woods to play.

"Mother says I'll be eaten by wolves," Gertie said.

"You won't," I said. "I've never been eaten by wolves, and I play in The Woods all the time."

"Don't you ever get lost? Mother is always afraid I'll lose my way."

"I'm never lost. I have a magic path." Gertie's eyes got as big as apples. Magic was rare, and my path was something special. It only appeared when I wanted it to, and it

3

led me wherever I wanted to go in The Woods. Surely this would entice Gertie to come with me, but it didn't. She stepped away from me. Her eyes grew wary.

"Mother says magic is dangerous."

"My path isn't dangerous," I said with indignation. "Granny made it to keep me safe. She made it grow right out of the ground after a bear attacked me and I almost died." I thought this would impress her. The possibility of death was always exciting, and being able to defy it with magic was even better.

"Mother says your granny is a witch," said Gertie.

Of course Granny was a witch. I knew that, but Gertie said it like it was a bad thing. Desperation took hold of me. I *really* wanted to play with Gertie in The Woods. So I did the only sensible thing I could think of. I cast the Worrywart Spell on Gertie's mother.

Worrywart Spell
Worry's a wart upon your chin
It spreads and grows from deep within
Make the wart shrink day by day
Send your worries far away

Unfortunately, the spell did nothing to cure Helga's worries. Instead, she grew a wart on her chin. The wart grew steadily bigger, day by day, until Granny was summoned to remedy my mistake. Needless to say, I wasn't allowed to play with Gertie anymore—or anyone else—for, in addition to being a worrywart, Helga was also the village gossip. The news spread all over The Mountain.

"She's a witch," Helga told the villagers, "just like her grandmother." She seemed to forget it was Granny who had cured her.

Gertie stopped talking to me, and no one else would even look at me. The magic in me grew hot and sticky. It coated my throat. It stung my eyes. I wished I could swallow it down and make it disappear.

"Don't worry, Red," Granny told me. "We all make mistakes. When I was your age, I tried to summon a rabbit to be my pet, and instead I called a bear to the door!"

"No!" I cried. "How did you survive?"

"The bear was actually quite nice. My sister married him."

"She married a *bear*?"

"Oh, don't be ridiculous. He wasn't really a bear. He was a prince under a spell."

This did nothing to alleviate my concerns. I didn't want to marry a bear *or* a prince.

"All the magic I do is bad," I said.

"Nonsense, child," said Granny. "They're only mistakes. It takes a hundred miles of mistakes before you arrive at your own true magic."

"But what if my mistakes are too big?"

"No such thing, dear," said Granny.

But she was wrong. I went on trying spells and charms and potions, and I went on making mistakes. Big ones. Small ones. Deadly ones.

My last mistake was worse than warts, fire, or roses out the nose.

I was seven years old, and Granny and I were in The

Woods. It was early spring, so the trees were just budding. Granny thought I could help them grow.

Growing Charm
Root in the earth
Sprout above ground
Swell in the sun
Spread all around

"What if I burn down The Woods?" I asked, trembling. Fire seemed to be the only magic I had a knack for.

"Don't be afraid, Red," said Granny. She pointed to a tree branch above us, a large one that dipped low enough that I could see the little branches and buds shooting out of it. "Focus on that branch. Feel its energy and the energy inside you. They are connected. See if you can make its leaves grow. Growing is the best kind of magic."

Yes, I loved it when Granny made things grow. She could grow juicy strawberries and fat pumpkins, spicy herbs and fragrant blossoms. Roses. Granny was particularly good with roses.

I focused on the magic inside me. I felt it swirling in my belly, like a bubbling pot of soup ready to spill over. I felt it flow through my arms and to the edges of my fingertips. Then I let the magic pour out of me and flow toward the tree. The buds on the branch swelled and started to unfurl. Nothing exploded. Nothing caught fire.

"I'm doing it!" I said.

"Good!" said Granny. "Keep going!"

Buds kept swelling, leaves unfurling, until the branch

was full of green and pink. Then the branch itself started to grow. It got thicker and longer.

"Slow it down now," said Granny. "Pull that magic back inside."

But I couldn't. The magic bubbled and spilled out of me faster than I could control it. The branch swelled and extended, too big and heavy for the tree. It sagged and creaked.

Everything happened at once.

The branch snapped. Granny pushed me out of the way. As I tumbled to the ground, so did the branch. There was a scream and a crash. When I looked up, Granny was on the ground, trapped under the branch.

Her eyes were closed and she was still.

"Granny?" I raced to her. I shook her shoulder, but she didn't wake. There was blood on her face, a trickle of red that seeped into the lines on her cheek. My heart pounded in my chest. I tried to pull the branch off her, but it was too big and I was too small.

I ran out of The Woods, tears blurring my vision so I could barely see my path. When I reached home, I burst through the door, sobbing.

"She's dead! I killed her! I killed Granny!"

Papa ran into The Woods. Mama held me in her arms as I curled into a ball and trembled like a sapling in a thunderstorm. I cried and cried. In my mind, I could see Granny, eyes closed, still as stone, and the blood on her face bright red. It was a message.

You did this, Red. You killed your granny.

Mama could not calm me.

When Papa returned, he got down low and whispered to me. "She's all right, Red. Just a few scratches and a hurt foot. She's just fine." I started crying anew, flooded with relief and sorrow. She was alive, but still I had hurt her. It was my fault.

Granny's foot never quite healed after that. She had to use a cane, and she hobbled like an old lady—like a witch. I hated to see it, but it reminded me every day of what I had done, what I was. Granny may have been a witch, but she was a good witch. Her magic made things live and grow. My magic made them bleed and die. It didn't matter if this was mile ninety-nine of my hundred miles of mistakes, I couldn't journey one step farther.

I would never do magic again.

CHAPTER TWO

The Path in The Woods

"Goodbye, Red! Take care of Granny!" Papa called as he smacked the reins on the mule.

I watched my parents bounce down The Mountain with a wagonload of logs to sell in The Valley, The Queen's City, Yonder, and Beyond, leaving me to stay with Granny.

"And stay on your path!" called Mama.

"I always do," I said, though she couldn't hear me. I waved one last goodbye before my parents disappeared around a bend, leaving only a trail of dust. They wouldn't be back for at least a week, perhaps two, which left Granny and me all alone in The Woods.

I was thrilled by the thought.

I heaved up my basket, full of fresh bread, salted pork, and a pot of honey. Granny didn't need any of it, but Mama insisted on sending something besides just me, as though I were a burden and Granny required compensation to take care of me.

I stepped into The Woods, and immediately the earth beneath me trembled. The leaves rustled and spread apart. The tree roots sank into the ground, and stones rose up out of the dirt, creating a path—my path—stretching straight into The Woods toward Granny's house.

I drank in the smell of pine and ripening earth. It was late summer, but there was a hint of spice in the air, foretelling autumn. The chatter of squirrels and birds and the buzz of insects all harmonized to compose a wild, rustic tune.

A crow landed on a branch near my head and made an off-key squawk, a complaint that he was hungry but couldn't find any mice.

"Well, what do you want me to do about it?" I said. "I don't have a magnificent beak like you, nor wings to fly."

He squawked in annoyance and flew away.

I can understand most creatures in The Woods—their chatter, their cries for food and shelter, or a mate. They don't have words, not like humans, but the meanings of their sounds and movements ripple through me. It's almost like a smell. Anyone can smell onions or basil and know exactly what it is, without words or sight. That's how it feels when the animals speak. They make a sound, and I know what it means. Granny says this is part of my magic. I say it's just proof of my beastly nature.

I came to the tree that marked the way to my honey hive. It leaned ever so slightly to the left, as if it were pointing the way. But today I passed it by. Granny was waiting, and I was eager to see her. I switched my cumbersome basket to the other arm and kept walking. I listened to the quarreling squirrels, the busy birds, and the munching rabbits, until they suddenly became quiet. A fawn leapt between the trees and galloped away. A flock of quail erupted from the brush and scattered in fear.

I stopped.

To my right, a shadow moved. Something big and powerful. I couldn't see it, but I could feel it. I stopped and listened. Something shifted on my left, and then the creature emerged through the trees, just a few feet from my path. He dipped his head, acknowledging me.

"Hello, wolf," I said. "Come to steal a pig?"

I'd seen this one a lot lately. He was big and black and, strangely, all alone. Last week one of Granny's pigs went missing, and I suspected it was this wolf who'd taken it.

He stepped closer, his big paw on the edge of my path.

The wolf looked up at me with big green eyes. He whined a little, like a pitiful pup.

Come, he said. He wanted me to let him come onto my path.

"Do I look like a fool to you?" I said. "You have very big teeth. Too big for my path."

The wolf whined a little more. I almost felt sorry for him.

"You're a wily one, aren't you?" I pulled out a chunk of salted pork and tossed it. The wolf caught the meat between his jaws and devoured it. "Well, what do you say?"

The wolf did not thank me. He never did, though I'd given him plenty of food in the past, offerings meant to keep him away from Granny's pigs and chickens.

The wolf whined again, pawing at the edge of my path. *Come.* That was all he ever said. *Come.* He pleaded for me to let him on my path or for me to leave my path and follow him. I wouldn't, of course, but part of me did wonder what it would be like to run through The Woods with a wolf. Wild. Exciting. Dangerous.

I wished the wolf would speak to me a little more at least. Other animals were simple, and I understood them simply, but not this wolf. I sensed his depth and complexity, a web of thought and emotions that I couldn't fully access. I believed he had words and thoughts every bit as intelligent as mine, and I wanted to know what they were.

Something deeper in the trees creaked. Leaves rustled. The wolf stiffened, then bolted away just as an arrow shot onto the edge of my path, right where the wolf had been.

An old man stumbled out of the trees. He held a bow and arrow and swung it around in all directions, searching for his prey. It was Horst the huntsman.

"Which way did he go?" Horst said in a ragged, breathy voice.

"Who?" I asked.

His eyes darted about. "The wolf. I saw him just now."

"He went that way," I said. "But I don't think you'll catch him."

Horst stomped his foot, and dust billowed off him. I'd never been this close to the huntsman before. "Old" was not the right word for him. He was ancient. His skin was ashen, his beard long and grizzled. He was covered head to foot in the skins and furs of all the beasts of The Woods, relics of his earlier days as a strong and able huntsman, though I doubted he could catch a rabbit now.

"I'll catch him," he said. "I'll catch him like I caught all the others. Got to use your brains, see." He pointed to his head. "Have to be patient. That wolf is a wily beast, full of tricks, but old Horst knows a thing or two." Horst lowered his bow and looked at me. He started, as though seeing me for the first time. "What are you doing in The Woods? This is no place for a little girl!"

"I'm here all the time," I said. "My granny lives in The Woods."

"Your granny?"

"Rose Red?"

"Oh, yes, the witch." He said "witch" casually, the way he might say "the baker" or "the miller." "I was thinking of paying her a visit," said Horst. "See if she can help me with this stiffness in my knee." He tried to move his knee around, and it creaked and cracked like a rusty hinge.

Granny was not fond of visitors. "I don't think—"

A rabbit sprang from a bush. Horst swung around and shot an arrow, but missed. "Rats!" He hobbled after the rabbit, muttering curses beneath his breath.

Poor Horst. He wasn't much of a huntsman.

I sighed and kept walking, switching the cursed basket to my other arm. Wolves and huntsmen. What next?

I watched for Granny's house to appear. Any minute now. I'd been to Granny's a thousand times, and still her house always seemed to appear out of nowhere. At first, all I could see was trees, and then, as I came closer, the trees grew together and changed shape, and then there was Granny's cottage, moss dangling from the roof, ivy creeping up the walls, smoke rising from the chimney. Roses blossomed all around the cottage, and thick trees stood on each side of the door, like sentinels keeping watch.

I knocked on the door. "Granny? It's me, Red."

"Come in, child. It's not locked."

I opened the door and stepped into the familiar smell of warm spices and fresh growing things. The ceiling was hung with herbs and flowers, the table and shelves covered with little clay pots and jars and pestle and mortar for potion making. Granny's rocking chair sat close to the fireplace, with a rabbit-fur rug on the floor for me. This was where we usually sat when Granny told me stories.

But Granny was not in her chair.

"Granny?"

A rustling sound came from the other side of the cottage, near Granny's bed. I went closer and gave a little yelp. There, in Granny's bed, wearing Granny's nightgown and nightcap, was a wolf.

CHAPTER THREE

Wolf Granny

"Why, hello, Red," said the wolf. "Don't you look tasty—I mean, lovely today."

"Oh, Granny," I said. "What big eyes you have!"

"The better to see you with, my dear," said the wolf. "Come closer, will you?"

I stepped closer. "Granny, what big ears you have!"

"The better to hear you with, my dear. Come just a little closer."

I stepped right beside the bed. "Oh, Granny! What big *teeth* you have!"

"The better to eat you with!"

The wolf opened its jaws and swallowed my head. I shrieked until its teeth tickled my neck, and then I laughed. Finally the wolf stopped and let me go. It reached up with hairy paws and pulled off its head, revealing Granny underneath. She smacked her lips. "You were delicious."

Sometimes Granny used a wolf disguise to scare un-wanted visitors away. I was generally a wanted visitor, so someone must have come recently.

"Who was it this time?" I asked.

"Oh, just some chatty girl."

Granny received a steady stream of visitors who wanted their fortunes told, or magical cures for whatever ailments they had. The wolf costume was a quicker way to be rid of people than trying to explain that magic didn't always do what you wanted it to.

"This girl would not go away," said Granny. "She knocked and knocked and chattered endlessly about needing some potion. Finally I had to turn myself into a wolf. Otherwise, I probably would have turned *her* into a mouse."

I laughed. "You couldn't turn her into a mouse! You wouldn't!"

"I could and I would," said Granny. "Here, watch. I'll show you. The spell goes like this:

"Squeak and skitter, tiny critter—"

"Stop!" I cried. "I don't want to be a mouse!"

Granny looked offended. "I wasn't going to turn *you* into a mouse. I was going to turn Milk into a mouse."

There was a *clip-clop* on the wooden floor.

Mmmmaa-aaaa-aa.

A goat was tethered to the foot of Granny's bed, chew-ing on some fresh clover.

"Why is Milk in the house?"

Milk was an old nanny goat who no longer gave milk, but Granny kept her around anyway. Milk used to belong to my friend Rump, but then he left The Mountain to go on his own adventures. Before he left, he gave Granny the goat, and she'd become a sort of pet.

"I couldn't leave her outside by herself," said Granny. "There's a monster in The Woods. They took another pig."

"Another pig?" Curse that wolf! That was the second this month. I shouldn't have given him any pork. Clearly he'd eaten already. I'd have words for him next time. Or stones.

"I met a wolf prowling not too far from here. Perhaps you should bring the pigs in the house, too."

"Not enough room," said Granny. "I can spare the pigs, but not Milk. She's a good guard goat."

"A guard goat?" The goat bit into a lump of hay and chewed noisily.

"Yes, she warns me when intruders are coming. She warned me about you."

"I'm not an intruder!"

Mmmaaaa-aaaa-aaaaa.

"You are to *her*," said Granny, laughing, and then her laugh turned into a cough. She blew her nose into her handkerchief, her hands still disguised as wolf paws.

"Are you sick?" I asked.

"Well, I'm no songbirdaaa . . . *aaaAAACHIPMUNKS!*" Granny sneezed. Her voice sounded stuffy and scratchy. "Did you need something?"

"I've come to stay with you, remember? Mama and Papa are gone."

"Oh. Yes, yes, of course I remember. I just forgot. Come, let's make some supper."

Granny slid out of bed, a furry tail she had attached to her nightgown sticking out behind her. She snapped her fingers and started a fire. I carried the kettle.

While I pulled water from the well, Granny pulled carrots from the ground, growing them an extra inch or two as they came out. While I chased a chicken with a stick, Granny brushed the dainty white buds of her strawberry patch, and they swelled and blushed into juicy red berries. While I plucked the feathers from the chicken, Granny plucked a sprig of rosemary and multiplied it into three.

Granny, much like a mother hen, clucked at my pitiful plucking. "Red, dear, you know there are better methods for this." She waved her hands over the chicken, magically removing all the feathers I hadn't managed to pull. "Chop some vegetables, will you?"

I got the kitchen knife and painstakingly chopped carrots and onions. My eyes watered from the onions.

"Don't cry, dear," said Granny. "It's so unnecessary." She whispered a spell to the knife, and within seconds the vegetables were perfectly chopped.

Sometimes I really wished I could do magic. I wished my magic could be like Granny's. She performed her spells without causing any mayhem. Her magic never harmed anyone. It made everything better. Granny made the whole world wonderful.

Soon the soup bubbled, and the air smelled of delicious herbs and onions. I got the spoons while Granny served the soup. She swooped her hands in the air, and the ladle dipped itself in the pot and scooped the steaming soup into our bowls. But on the second bowl, the ladle faltered. The bowl toppled from the table and broke in two, splattering soup all over.

"Oh, dear." Granny swayed a little and leaned against the table.

I rushed to her. "What's wrong?"

She clasped my arm. Her hands were cold and clammy, despite the warmth from the fire. "I think I overdid it," she said. "I'm not the sprightly witch I once was." She tried to laugh but ended up coughing instead.

"Maybe you should lie down." I tried to lead her to her bed.

Granny waved me away. "I'm just famished, is all. I forgot breakfast when that silly girl came nosing around. Let's eat." I cleaned up the mess while Granny ladled the soup without magic, using just her own two hands. They trembled ever so slightly.

We slurped our soup and ate bread spread thick with butter and honey, followed by the juicy strawberries.

"I spotted a dwarf yesterday," said Granny.

I dropped my spoon. "You did? Where?" I had never seen a dwarf. Very few people ever had, but Granny encountered one when she was twelve, same age as me, and her stories made me eager to find one myself.

"I saw him close to the stream. I tried to follow him, but he disappeared down a hole. In my younger years, I would have caught him."

"I can't understand it," I said. "I've searched for

dwarves for ages, and yet you spot one on a morning walk!" I shoved a strawberry in my mouth.

"Just as well," said Granny. "Dwarves are crabby, crotchety creatures, secretive and reclusive. They detest humans. Most dwarves go their entire lives without ever coming aboveground. That's why so few humans ever see one."

"I'll see one," I said, determined. "I've seen a fair few things most humans haven't."

"If you do, keep that hidden." She pointed to the ruby ring I wore around my neck. Granny had given it to me when I was born. It was supposed to remind me that my name held beauty and magic—or some such nonsense.

"Why?" I asked.

"Dwarves love rubies. They love all gems, but rubies are their favorite. They'll steal it from you if they see it. Probably gives them loads of magic."

I clutched at the ring. Dwarf magic is powerful indeed, according to Granny. They know where everything is, and their underground tunnels go everywhere: The Kingdom, The Mountain, Yonder, and Beyond. They know every landmark, and they know where to find things. Powerful things. Secret things. Things you never knew existed. Dwarves are little traveling wizards. If you're ever lost or need to find something, a dwarf can set you straight, but only if you take them by the beard. If you take a dwarf by the beard, they have to do whatever you say, take you wherever you want to go, and tell you whatever you wish to know.

"One day you'll catch a dwarf," said Granny, "and he'll show you all sorts of secret, magical things. But be warned—dwarves can be nasty little tricksters."

"It doesn't matter," I said, trying to sound as though I didn't care. "I have you, and you know more than dwarves."

"Huh. I won't be around forever," said Granny. She coughed into her sleeve. "Get me some water, would you? I'm parched."

I poured a cup of water. Her hands trembled as she lifted the cup to her mouth.

"You're really sick, aren't you?" I said.

"Do you think I'm playacting?"

"No, it's just . . ." I trailed off. It was just that Granny was never sick. For as long as I could remember, she hadn't suffered so much as a runny nose, and she had a potion to cure every ailment. Last winter I became so ill I could barely breathe, so Granny gave me her Curious Cure-All, a slimy green concoction that tasted like poison, but I was better the next day.

Of course. That was all Granny needed.

"Where's your Curious Cure-All?" I asked.

"Gone," said Granny. "You had the last spoonful last winter, remember?"

Of course. It *would* be my fault.

"Can't you make more?" I asked.

Granny shook her head. "Not when I'm sick. Difficult ingredients, though *you* could make it."

I stiffened. "You know I can't."

"I know no such thing, and I fancy I know quite a lot. For instance, I know I'm cold. Build up the fire, will you?" She pulled her shawl over her shoulders.

I put more wood on the fire, then felt her forehead. "You're very warm."

"No, cold," Granny muttered.

"Perhaps you should go back to bed. I'll clean up."

Granny coughed, and crawled into bed, her wolf tail still attached to her nightgown. I washed and dried the dishes, scrubbed the pot, then swept the floor. If Granny had been well, it all would have been done much faster. She had a very good spell that could make the broom sweep by itself.

Sweeping Spell
Broom awake
Shoo the dirt
Clear the floor
Beneath my skirt

I had tried it once. The broom attacked me. And maybe broke a few things.

When everything was clean and put away, I sat in Granny's rocking chair and listened to the rasp of her breathing. It was nothing, I told myself. Just a little cold. She would be better in the morning.

CHAPTER FOUR

A Red Gift

Granny was not better in the morning. She was worse. She burned with fever and shivered with chills. She coughed and coughed and coughed.

"You need your Curious Cure-All," I said.

"The ingredients are listed on the table," she said in a raspy voice.

I went to the table. Granny had all her potion and medicine recipes carved directly into the wood, a jumble of words etched on the top and the legs and even underneath. She said she couldn't lose them that way.

I searched the table. There was a recipe for curing baldness (2 scoops of troll droppings and 1 fuzzy caterpillar) and one for rashes and bites (3 sprigs of lavender, 2 drops of frog slime, and 2 spits from a witch, though any spit will suffice).

Finally I found it.

Curious Cure-All

5 prickly chestnuts

1 handful of wild cherries

1 bunch of gnomeswort

So far, these ingredients would be easy to find. I read on.

1 drop of pixie venom (wear gloves)

"Pixie venom!" I shouted. "For medicine?"

"Powerful stuff," said Granny.

Undoubtedly. One bite from a pixie was as painful as a hundred bee stings.

1 pair of tree-nymph wings

"How am I supposed to tell the nymph wings from leaves?" I asked.

"You have to pluck them right off the tree nymph," she said. "Otherwise, they don't work."

"Isn't that a bit cruel?"

"They grow back," she croaked. "They don't mind."

Even if I could find a tree nymph, I'd never be able to catch it. I'd tried many times without success, but that seemed a small concern when I saw the last ingredient:

7 wolf hairs

"Can I get some wolf fur from your tail?"

"It's rabbit. Besides, wolf fur is best when it's fresh. Just ask nicely."

"Ask who?"

"A wolf, of course. Who else?"

I sighed. Sometimes Granny could be exasperating. She said crazy things as though they were completely normal and then made you feel crazy for thinking what she said was crazy. Asking questions only made it worse.

"Is the wolf fur an essential ingredient?" I asked.

"Of course it's essential, otherwise it wouldn't be on the list of ingredients. Now stop asking me silly questions. It's giving me a headache." I abandoned the Curious Cure-All recipe and instead made lavender honey tea to soothe Granny's cough. I placed the cup to her lips, but she barely drank. I tried pressing cold cloths to her burning forehead, but she tossed and turned and talked nonsensically.

"Snow?" said Granny. "Is that you?" Snow was her sister, who had died long ago.

"Granny, it's me. Red."

"Red," said Granny. "I was Red once. Rose Red, they called me. Oh, I was beautiful. Just gorgeous. Everybody said so."

"You're still gorgeous," I said.

"Ha." She began to laugh, but then coughed, and the pain of it seemed to bring her back to awareness. "Oh, Red, it's you," Granny whispered, as though seeing me for the first time. "Happy birthday."

"It's not my birthday," I said.

"Of course it isn't. It's mine."

Granny's birthday? She had never mentioned it before, not once, but of course she had one. Why had I never considered it? She just seemed timeless somehow, like she always stayed the same age.

"I have a present for you," said Granny.

"You have a present for me on *your* birthday?"

Granny lifted her arm and pointed to the end of her bed. "Open that chest," she whispered.

I went to the big wooden chest at the foot of Granny's bed. I had gone through it many times. It was where she kept her treasures, as she called them, mostly from her childhood—crocheted baby bonnets; a patchwork quilt, worn and faded from many picnics; a white glove; dried roses that had once been red, now black and brittle; a miniature painting of Granny in a red cloak and her sister in a white one.

"What am I supposed to find?" I asked.

"Unfold the quilt," said Granny. "It's inside there."

I unfolded the quilt and something slid out onto the ground. It was bright red.

When I picked it up, the fabric unraveled like liquid, no wrinkles or folds. It was a cloak. A red cloak with a hood, just like the one Granny wore in the little painting.

"It was mine when I was your age," said Granny. "Put it on."

I hesitated.

"Go on. It won't bite you."

I wasn't so sure. I draped the cloak loosely over my shoulders. Granny motioned for me to come to her, and with trembling hands she fastened the clasp at my chest and pulled the hood over my head.

"Let me look at you," said Granny. "Ah, you look just like me when I was a girl."

I shifted uncomfortably.

"It's almost as if I'm young again, seeing you in that old thing. I had suitors coming through the front door before I could shove the last one out the back. My sister, Snow, had a matching white cloak, of course, and we wore them everywhere we went. Everyone called us Snow White and Rose Red."

Granny's sister, Snow, was the one who married the bear—not to be confused with the princess Snow White, who lived with dwarves while hiding from an evil queen. That Snow White had lived over two hundred years ago, but her name was a popular one. Anyone named Snow or Snow White had a destiny that usually involved dwarves or apples or sleeping curses. You never knew what you were going to get.

"We wore our cloaks wherever we went," said Granny. "We believed they were magic."

I stiffened. I wanted the cloak off me. "What kind of magic?"

But she didn't answer my question, not directly. "Red is a magical color. Powerful. When you were born, I knew that you were Red. I knew you had powerful magic in you."

I pulled at the cloak. It felt hot and suffocating.

"Don't take it off," said Granny. "It's going to get cold soon."

"It's summer," I said. "And it's very warm in here."

She closed her eyes and sniffed. "I can smell the cold coming."

"Your nose has always been a little off compared to the rest of your senses. It's too small." I tried to laugh at the joke, but it didn't come out right. Nothing felt right. Not this red cloak. Not this frail and fevered Granny. Not the world.

"Red." Granny clasped my hand. "Don't be afraid."

"I'm not afraid," I lied. "You just need to rest, and you need some medicine. One of your potions should make you better in an instant. Isn't there anything else you can take besides your Curious Cure-All?" I walked to the cupboard and started to rummage again. I found a clay pot full of greenish-brown goop. It smelled ghastly, but those were usually the potions that did the best curing. "How about this one?"

"Troll droppings. That will certainly finish me off," she said.

I replaced the pot and washed my hands. Granny coughed some more. It got worse each time.

"It's all right, Red," she croaked. "Sometimes we just need to let nature take its course."

"And sometimes we need to help it along with a little magic. You always say that."

"Yes, but magic can't help everything. You always say that."

"But you're very sick. Don't you want to get better?"

"No one lives forever," said Granny.

"Stop avoiding the question. Don't you want to get better?"

"Stop avoiding the truth." Granny grasped me by the arm, and the sudden firmness of her grip startled me more than her recent frailty.

"Everybody dies, Red," said Granny. "One way or another, everybody dies."

"I know," I said, but the words were thick in my mouth. They felt wrong. It wasn't at all like Granny to speak of death. She was magic, full of power and life. She couldn't be dying.

And yet the words echoed in my mind, lashing me with barbed whips.

Everybody dies.

Granny drifted to sleep. Her breathing was labored and raspy. My own breathing grew short and heavy. My throat swelled. My eyes burned. I couldn't stay here. Granny needed her Curious Cure-All, and it was up to me to make it.

I found Granny's sturdy gloves, a vial for the pixie venom, a net for catching nymphs, and a jar to hold the wolf fur. I placed all these things in my basket. Milk bleated at each of my movements, clearly concerned with my rush.

"I'll be back soon," I said. "Watch after Granny, will you?"

Maaaaaaa.

She said she would.

I took one last look at Granny. She'd get well. I might get bitten by pixies or eaten by a wolf, but Granny would not die.

CHAPTER FIVE
Curious Cure-All

The best place to find a pixie on The Mountain was the mines where we used to dig for gold.

I walked through the ruins of the village, past abandoned houses, the crumbling mill, the vacant square. All of it used to be full of people, loud and bustling, but not anymore. The only sound was the whisper of the wind scattering dust and leaves. We were alone on The Mountain, which was fine by me. Granny was all I needed.

This mine could hardly be called a mine anymore. Most of the shafts had collapsed, so you couldn't even walk in them. Abandoned carts and rusty pickaxes were strewn about on the ground. Someone had left a hat. It was caked with dust, and moldy from rain.

I saw no pixies, probably because there was no gold. Pixies love gold. They sense it from miles away and go crazy whenever they're near it. These mines used to be crawling with pixies—I used to swat them away like bugs. But now that I wanted to find one, there were none.

I searched along the sluices, where small children used to scoop up mud in pans and search for specks of gold. Most of the sluice boxes were broken and tipped over. I lifted some pieces off the ground, searching, and finally something colorful and sparkly fluttered beneath one of the boxes. A pixie!

She was nestled in a nest woven of grass and twigs and flecked with gold. I pulled on my leather gloves and poked at her. She squeaked and flew up to the sky, out of reach. I picked up a bit of her gold. She shrieked and darted back to bite my glove, digging her fangs into the leather. I dropped the gold, and the pixie snatched it and flew away again, this time out of sight. She had left behind a sizable drop of pixie venom. If she had bitten my bare hand, my finger would be as big as a sausage by now. I took the little vial from my apron pocket and squeezed the venom over the rim.

There! That wasn't so difficult. One ingredient found. Two to go.

I walked along my path toward my honey hive, searching for a good nymph tree. Tree nymphs are like pixies, but with twigs for bodies and leaf-wings that change with the seasons—green in the spring and summer, red and orange in the fall, brittle brown in the winter. They're so well disguised that few know of their existence. Some people swear that trees can speak, but they're really just hearing the tree nymphs trying to tell them something they forgot. Granny says when we forget something, the tree nymphs sweep up our memories and take care of them until we remember. I must not have forgotten anything important, because I've never understood a thing from the tree nymphs. They sound like rustling leaves to me.

The trick to spotting tree nymphs is to watch the movement of the leaves when a wind comes. When the wind rushes, all the leaves move, of course, but the nymphs will detach from their branches and flutter to other limbs or trees. Through this method I found some nymphs in an enormous beech tree with low-hanging limbs. I shook some of the branches until the nymphs floated down. I swished the net, but they evaded me, and all I caught was regular leaves. I tried again and again, swishing the net as fast as I could, but the nymphs swirled over my head, higher and higher in the tree.

I wasn't going to let that stop me. I put the net between my teeth and swung myself up into the tree, snagging my skirt in the process. Cursed skirt! I yanked it free, and it tore all the way to my knee. The leaves rustled. I could have sworn the nymphs were laughing at me.

I reached for the branch above me and shook it vigorously, waving my net as the nymphs detached.

"Ha! Gotcha!" And then I lost my balance and dropped the net. It clattered through the branches and fell to the ground while my hair got caught in a clump of beechnut burs.

"Aaaargh!" I growled. I tried to get free, twisting this

way and that, but only managed to get more tangled. And, of course, all my thrashing frightened the nymphs, so they flew farther up the tree, snickering in their secret language, while I remained hopelessly stuck.

This was not going as smoothly as I had planned.

A squirrel passed by, collecting nuts.

"*Pssst!* Squirrel! Some help?" I asked, pointing to my hair. "There are some very tasty nuts beneath all this mess, if you can help me out."

The squirrel regarded me for a moment, then chattered a lecture about how I had gotten myself into this fix, so I could get myself out.

Squirrels are selfish creatures, if you ask me. No help at all.

I went to work on my hair, ripping my tangles loose from the spiny burs, which pricked and scratched my hands. If I'd had some scissors, I'd have cut all my hair off right then. It's not as though I was trying to look special for anyone.

With a final yank, I was free.

I was also falling.

I plummeted headfirst to the ground. I hit branch after branch, until the hood of my cloak caught on one, saving me just in time. Blessed cloak!

I flipped over and hopped to the ground, miraculously in one piece but without a nymph. Perhaps tree climbing was not the best method for catching tree nymphs.

A wind picked up, and I shivered a little. The trees whispered, or the nymphs, and then my stomach grumbled, shouting at me for food. I'd been searching for nymphs and pixies all morning. I knew exactly where I'd go for lunch.

My honey hive.

My path immediately stretched in a new direction. This one curved and wound in and out of the trees and brush, which got thicker and thicker, until it all opened up to a small clearing. A gentle humming grew with each step, until it was a full buzzing chorus of a thousand bees. Music to my ears.

This was my honey hive. This was my place to think and be alone.

Except I wasn't alone.

Snap!

There was something near the hive. A brown figure moving around just outside the swarm of bees. *Bear,* I thought. Bears like honey, but they don't necessarily like little girls. I waited by a tree, listening for the bear to leave.

"Oh! Ouch! Ah! Get awayayayaaaah!"

Bears don't talk in squeaky little-girl voices, either. I peered around the tree, squinting to get a better view. Indeed, there was no bear, but a girl. She had covered herself in a brown shawl to serve as a shield from the bees.

Curses. I'd much rather face a bear.

CHAPTER SIX
Nosy Girl with Golden Curls

The bees swarmed the girl, trying to drive out the intruder. "Ah! Ouch!" she cried. "Why are you being so mean? What did I ever do to you?" She backed out of the buzzing mob and pulled her shawl off her head.

I knew this girl. She was about my age, maybe a little younger, but I clearly remembered the day her family had come to The Mountain to mine gold, eager and confident, though none of us understood why. We rarely found gold, and what we did find always went to the king, who gave us little more than survival in return. But then the father had proudly presented his daughter, a petite, dimple-cheeked girl with a headful of golden curls tucked in a frilly cap.

"This is my daughter, Goldie," he said. The rest of the grown-ups scratched their heads, wondering why in the name of The Mountain they hadn't thought to give their children *that* name. It seemed an obvious choice. A girl named Goldie was destined to find gold. And yet this name did not serve their family well, for it wasn't long before The Mountain ran dry of gold. We stopped receiving rations from the king, and when the king died, the new queen had no love for gold, and the mines were closed. Everyone left to find other trades and livelihoods—to be farmers or soldiers or merchants.

I thought Goldie and her family had moved away months ago with all the rest, but here she was, sticking her nose where it was not wanted.

"I just want a bit of honey, you know. I'm not here to hurt you!" She scolded the bees and swatted at them with her brown shawl. I rolled my eyes. Why did everyone think swatting at bees was a good idea?

"Ouch!" She threw up her hands in defeat. "Fine! Keep your stinking honey! It's probably disgusting anyway!" She kicked dirt at the bees and stomped off. I let out a breath and stepped into the clearing, glad to have it to myself again.

I approached the swarm of bees calmly, as light as a feather floating on a gentle breeze. A few bees came and landed on my ears and shoulders and head. I didn't flinch, and they didn't sting. I've never been stung, not even when I've taken their honey. Granny says it's because they can feel my magic and it makes them calm, which I find odd, since my magic makes *me* so uneasy.

I reached into the log and pulled out a lump of honeycomb, dripping and oozing with honey—and bees, of course. The red cloak was almost completely covered with bees. I stepped away from the hive, waiting until most of the bees flew away. Then I turned and froze.

Goldie was back. She stared at me, wide-eyed. She had rich brown eyes that stood out against her golden curls, and an innocent look about her that most people probably found sweet, but I was not fooled. I knew that the sweetest-looking creatures could also be the most vicious. And annoying. Pixies, for instance.

Her gaze shifted to the honey dripping down my hands. She licked her lips.

"How did you *do* that?" she said. "I tried for nearly an hour to get some honey, but those bees were such beasts! I couldn't get within a foot of the hive."

"That's because it's not yours," I said coldly.

"Oh, goodness, is it yours? Mummy is always scolding me for getting into other people's things, but I never suspected a *beehive* might belong to someone. Does it have your name on it?"

"I thought your family left The Mountain," I said, ignoring her questions.

"We did. Only I had to come back because I forgot something very important. I'm looking for—"

"How did you find this place?" I interrupted. I didn't care a bee's stinger what she was looking for.

"Oh, it was easy. I have a knack for finding things that are golden, of course. It's part of my destiny. Which reminds me, I've always wanted to ask you about *your* destiny. Red. It's a strange name. Everyone says it's evil. They say you're a witch. Are you?"

Goldie looked eager, like a witch was some exotic

animal she'd always wanted to see. I shifted uncomfortably. The honey continued to drip over my fingers and down my arm. Goldie eyed it hungrily. Maybe if I gave it to her, she'd go away. I held out the dripping honeycomb. "Here."

"Oh, how kind of you." Goldie took the honeycomb and licked it. "Mmmm! That is so good." She licked all the honey off her fingers and palms and then ate the comb itself, much like a bear would. "Thank you," she said. "That was just what I needed."

I thought she would leave then, but she didn't. She made herself comfortable on a nearby stump and spread her brown shawl around her. This was *my* hive and my honey. I wanted her gone. Now.

"You have to go now," I said.

"Why?"

"Because of the bees. They might try to sting you again."

"They're not stinging anymore. Now that you're here. *You* must be a bee charmer. Is that part of your destiny?"

"Yes," I said. "Now leave, or I'll set the bees on you."

Goldie's eyes widened, but with interest instead of fear. "Can you do that? Can you make them do what you want?"

"Yes," I lied. I could do no such thing.

Goldie licked her fingers and stood up. "Show me," she said. "Make them do something, but don't set them on me. Make them do something else."

"I'm not going to make them do anything," I said.

"But you can, can't you?"

I rolled my eyes, then had a stroke of genius. I pointed behind Goldie and feigned terror. "Bear!" I shouted.

Goldie whipped around. "Where?"

"It's coming this way. It wants the honey. Run for your life!"

Goldie shrieked and jumped up. She started to run and, unfortunately, grabbed my hand to tug me along with her. "Faster, Red! It's going to eat us!"

What could I do? I had to run from an imaginary bear.

We ran for a few minutes, then I pulled Goldie to a stop. "It's okay now. I think it went in the other direction."

She slumped against a tree. "I thought we were going to be *eaten*," she gasped. "There are so many frightful creatures in The Woods. Yesterday I tried to find The Witch of The Woods, but when I got to her house, there was a wolf! It was wearing a nightdress! Do you think it ate the witch?"

Ah. So this was the chatty girl who had bothered Granny. I didn't really want to draw Goldie into a conversation, but I couldn't help myself. "Maybe. What did you want from the witch?"

Goldie sighed. "A love potion."

Of course. Goldie had probably fallen in love with some silly boy who didn't like her back, so she ran away from home in search of a love spell. It was a common tale that always ended badly.

"You don't want a love spell," I told her.

"Of course I do. I *need* it."

"Magic doesn't always turn out the way you expect."

"What do you mean?"

I sighed. No one ever considered the consequences.

"If you were to get a love spell, it might work, but it might do other things, too, like make the person you love very sick." Once, a girl named Nancy gave a love potion to Hans Jacob, and it made him so sick he couldn't even propose, he was so busy retching. Granny gave him an antidote, which made Nancy furious.

"I should love for someone to be lovesick over me," sighed Goldie.

"Or it could make them extremely ugly."

Goldie's cheek twitched, but she stuck out her chin and said, "That doesn't matter to me. Mummy says real beauty is on the inside."

I was not being forceful enough. I needed to think of the worst consequence possible. It came to me quickly. "It could kill the one you love," I said gravely. "A spell, especially a strong one like a love spell, can be *too* much for someone to endure, and they could die. So could you."

"Oh," said Goldie, "yes, that would be terrible." I thought I had gotten to her at last, but after a moment she perked up. "But there's a risk in everything, isn't there? And I'd risk everything for love. Even death! Wouldn't you?"

I didn't reply. A leaf fluttered in front of me and then swirled away. No, not a leaf. A nymph! I followed it.

"Where are you going?" asked Goldie.

"Nowhere," I said, keeping my eyes locked on the nymph. It was so close I could see its twiggy legs, the slight fuzz on its leaflike wings, yellow with red tinges on the edges.

"It's a very pretty leaf," said Goldie. "Red and gold always look so lovely together, don't you think?"

"It's not a leaf," I said. "It's a nymph." The nymph landed on a stone covered with moss. I moved silently and hovered over the stone. The nymph opened and closed its wings.

"Great gourds!" shouted Goldie just as I pounced, and the nymph flew away. "Did you see that? It was *alive*! It had legs and eyes!"

"Yes," I said, grinding my teeth. "I told you, it's a tree nymph."

"I've never seen one before, or if I have, I always thought it was a leaf. Did you want it for a pet?"

"No. I need its wings."

"What for?"

"To make a potion."

"A potion! What kind of potion?"

"One to give boils to people who get on my nerves." I glared at her.

Goldie screwed up her face. "That doesn't sound as nice as a love potion, but I'll help you catch it."

"No thank you," I said, and started walking as quickly as possible. I wound in and out of the trees to try to get rid of Goldie, but all that seemed to accomplish was to confuse my path as it tried to anticipate my movements. Goldie skipped right alongside me. When she got too close to my path, she got a small shock that made her jump and stumble sideways. She batted at the air.

"I think there are still bees following me. Where are we going again?"

"*I* need to catch a tree nymph," I said, hoping she would get the hint that *we* weren't going anywhere. No such luck.

"Right," Goldie said in a determined voice. "Nymphs for boils. Oh, look! There's one!" Goldie pointed right behind me.

"That's only a leaf," I said.

"No! It's right by your head!"

I kept still. I felt wings brushing ever so gently against my cheek, and then the nymph crawled into my hair right by my ear. It made strange little sounds, a series of clicks and soft whistling, like wind through a crack in the door. It was saying something. I strained to understand.

"Don't move," said Goldie. "I got it. I'm very good at catching grasshoppers." She crouched, ready to pounce like a cat.

"No. Don't—"

Goldie sprang toward me. My path exuded a blast of air so strong that Goldie's frilly cap blew clean off her head and she tumbled to her rear. But the blast scared off the nymph, too.

Goldie shook herself. "Great gourds, what a wind! That came out of nowhere. Didn't you feel it?"

I clenched my teeth and my fists. It was taking every ounce of my control not to punch Goldie in the nose. I'd punched people for lesser offenses. I spun around and started walking fast, but Goldie ran to keep up with me and chattered away.

"Don't worry. I'm sure we can catch another. We just

have to keep trying. Mummy always says you should never give up. Unless, of course, you're doing something *wrong*, in which case you should give up entirely, and it has occurred to me that trying to make a potion to give people boils could be wrong, don't you think?"

"I'm not trying to poison people!" I blurted. "I needed those nymph wings to make a medicine for my granny, who is ill." I trembled with rage, but Goldie mistook it for sadness.

"Oh, Red." She reached out and took hold of my hands. "I am *so* sorry. My granny died when I was little, and I cried and cried."

I tore my hands out of her grasp and folded my arms. The last thing I wanted was for Goldie to think she understood me. "She's not dying," I said. "And I never cry."

"Don't worry," said Goldie. "My mummy always knows what to do in these situations. Maybe your mummy would know what to do?"

As much as I didn't want to take any help or advice from Goldie, she had a point. Mama and Papa would know what to do. If I could find a gnome to take them a message, then they'd come home. They could be back by nightfall.

I ran through the trees so fast my path could barely keep up with me, and I spooked the birds and other creatures, who scattered before me, twittering warnings.

"Message!" I called. "Message!" I shouted as loud as I could into bushes and burrows. These were the most likely places to find gnomes, but like pixies, they had mostly fled The Mountain. They preferred to live near crowds, where they could deliver lots of messages. But there had to be at least one!

"I NEED TO SEND A MESSAGE NOW, YOU STUPID GNOMES!" I stomped my foot and punched a tree, which accomplished nothing, but hurt my hand.

"Are you trying to catch a gnome now? I can help."

"I don't need help," I said.

"I'm really good at finding gnomes," she said.

"Good for you. Message!" I called again.

"Message!" Goldie echoed. "I think we'd do better if we went this way." She pointed toward the stream.

I nodded. "Go ahead, then," I said. Goldie skipped ahead, while I turned and quickly went in the other direction.

"Oh, look! I found one!"

I nearly crashed into a tree to stop myself. I whipped around and ran back toward Goldie. "Where?" I asked.

"There!" Goldie pointed toward some tall grass.

"I don't see—"

The grass moved. Then it grunted. A head bobbed above it.

Gnome!

I lunged forward and snatched up the gnome by the scruff of his neck. The gnome immediately started kicking and grunting, which is normal behavior for gnomes until you tell them you want them to send a message. Then they calm down and listen.

"I want to send a message to my parents, Agnes and Thomas."

But the gnome did not calm down. "Lemme go! Lemme go!" He thrashed and flailed his little limbs, and then he bit me.

"Ouch!" I let go and he fell to the ground. There were teeth marks on my pointer finger. Blood dripped down my hand. Never, ever would a gnome bite a person who wanted to send a message.

I looked down at the creature and inspected him more closely. He was slightly bigger than most gnomes, and his features were sharp and shrewd. He was all points: pointy nose, pointy ears, pointy beard. He wore a pointy hat, too, and long, pointy shoes. He glared at me, pointedly, with dark intelligent eyes. This was not the blank stare of a gnome.

"You're a dwarf!" I said.

"And you're a big ugly girl!" The dwarf kicked me in the shin and ran away.

CHAPTER SEVEN

By the Beard

I rubbed my shin and pressed my bleeding hand into my apron. I'd searched for a dwarf for years, but my first encounter was not as magical as I'd imagined. Little brute!

"A dwarf!" Goldie was astonished. "I've never seen a dwarf before! He wasn't very friendly, was he?"

No. He wasn't. But then I remembered what Granny had taught me about dwarves. If you caught one by the beard, it had to do whatever you asked—guide you wherever you wished to go.

I sucked in my pain and ran after the dwarf.

"Where are you going?" Goldie asked.

"To catch a dwarf!"

"Goodness, you certainly like chasing things, don't you?"

I ignored Goldie and instead focused on my pursuit. Curses, the dwarf was fast! Much faster than a gnome. I chased him over a rock and around a tree. I leapt over shrubs. He was just about to escape down a hole when I dove and caught him by the foot. The dwarf spat insults and tried to bite me again, until I grasped him by his pointy black beard.

"Lemme go! Gerroff! Gerroff, you stinking human!" He flailed and twisted and kicked, but I held fast to his beard. What now? Was there something I had to say? A spell or incantation? Granny had never said.

"Oh, Dwarf," I proclaimed. "I take thee by the beard and—er—request your assistance on my journey."

The dwarf stopped his flailing. He turned red as a radish and glared at me. "You nasty little witch!" He took a small ax from his waist and smacked my arm with the flat side, right on my funny bone. I dropped the dwarf.

"Ouch! You little monster!" I rubbed my elbow and shook my arm.

The dwarf stood with his ax over his shoulder, glaring up at me as though he wanted to chop me to bits.

"I don't think he appreciated you grabbing his beard," Goldie whispered.

"What do you want?" the dwarf asked sharply.

"A love potion, please," said Goldie.

The dwarf eyed Goldie as though she were a cockroach. "I wasn't asking you." He turned back to me, impatiently waiting for my answer. I opened my mouth and shut it again.

Goldie's request gave me an idea. I had planned to ask the dwarf how to catch a nymph, but even if I succeeded in making the Cure-All, Granny could get sick again.

Everyone dies.

But did everyone *have* to die?

Granny always says that life is magic. Everyone has magic, even if they don't know it. Magic is what makes them alive. So if life is magic, and Granny was dying, then what was really dying was her magic. It was fading from her. But did it have to fade? What if that magic could be replenished? What if there was a way to live forever?

I'd seen death on The Mountain. I'd heard the bell chime thirteen times and the endless cries and wails of those who mourned the loss of loved ones. Some people never recovered from their grief. Some people were lost without their loved ones. Death was awful, and all these thoughts came down to one simple fact:

I didn't want Granny to die. Not ever.

And now I had within my grasp a possible key to saving her. Dwarves knew things. Secret things. Magic things.

"My granny is very sick," I began.

"I can give you directions to an apothecary, herbalist, physician—" The dwarf rattled off different options with a glazed expression.

"No," I interrupted, "I don't need any of those. I want to know . . . That is, could you possibly . . . Do you know of some magic that could keep someone alive? Forever?"

The dwarf's eyebrows rose to two sharp points. "Ah, death. The human tragedy. Your pitifully short existence is not enough for you. You fear *the end.*"

I put my hands on my hips. "I'm not afraid. I'm just trying to help my granny and you're not helping. You're supposed to do as I ask. Or do I need to snatch your beard again?"

The dwarf stepped back and grabbed his beard protectively. "Oh, begging your pardon, *master*," he said in a poisonous voice. "I *can* tell you of magic that could make you live forever, but it all depends on how far you're willing to go."

I thought of Granny, how miserable and alone I would be if I didn't have her. "To the ends of the earth," I said.

"That's what they all say," said the dwarf with a smile, but not a friendly one. His teeth were too large for his face. It made him look rather sinister. But I refused to be frightened of him. I had taken him by the beard, and he had to do as I said. He had to help.

"Tell me what you know," I commanded.

"Of course, of course," he said. "I know of three ways to stop death, but I am only obligated to direct you to one."

Three ways to stop death! This was fortunate. Even if I couldn't find one, or it didn't work for some reason, I could search for the others.

"Tell me," I said.

"The first magic can be found in a well," he began. "At first glance, it seems an ordinary well, except it contains not water but wine, red wine. Any who drink this wine will have their youth restored to them."

"That sounds lovely!" said Goldie. "Can you imagine always being young and beautiful?" Goldie sighed. I tried to ignore her and focus on what the dwarf had said.

A well of wine. I imagined Granny drinking wine that

brought back not only her strength but all her youth and beauty. She was always talking about how beautiful she used to be. Wouldn't she love to be young and beautiful again?

"The second magic," said the dwarf, "can be found at an enchanted castle. Within the very center of its garden are Red Roses. Magic roses that bloom all year round. Prick your finger on a thorn, give a drop of blood to the earth, and you will never die."

A rose. Yes. Granny's name was Rose Red. Red roses would suit her very well.

"I like roses," spouted Goldie, "but I shouldn't like to prick my finger. Mummy told me a story of a girl who pricked her finger and she fell asleep for a hundred years!"

"But that wasn't a rose, was it?" I said.

"No, it was a spindle, of course," said Goldie.

"Right. Thorns are different from spindles." I turned back to the dwarf, who was tapping his pointed shoe impatiently. "And the third magic?" I asked.

"It is called The Magic Hearts."

"Magic Hearts?" It sounded sappy, like something from old tales about how the best magic comes from the heart, but that wouldn't be useful to my situation.

The dwarf nodded. "Those who possess The Magic Hearts will never die, but only grow stronger. This magic is possibly the most powerful of the three."

Powerful. I did like the sound of that, but I needed to know more before I could decide. "Exactly how does one possess these hearts? Do you collect them like tokens or charms?"

The dwarf shrugged. "Few know of this magic's existence, and I cannot say where it is found. I can only tell you that it exists."

"Why tell me about it if you can't tell me where it is?"

"You demanded the information, so it is my obligation to tell you," the dwarf sneered.

"Um, excuse me, Mr. Dwarf," chirped Goldie, "but are these Magic Hearts by chance similar to a love potion? Because they sound very much like one."

The dwarf acted like he could neither see nor hear Goldie. "Now you must choose, *master*." His voice dripped with disdain. "To which magic shall I direct you?"

Which magic? Wine. Roses. Hearts. Each sounded equally promising and equally elusive. I liked the sound of The Wine Well, because Granny would love being young again. What if we could be girls together? She could be like my sister. We'd race through The Woods, climb trees, and talk to all the animals.

I liked the sound of the roses because Granny loved roses, and she was Rose. It made sense, but what if she had to pick the rose herself for it to work? And The Magic Hearts . . . the dwarf said they were the most powerful of the three, but I had no idea what I'd be searching *for*, and he said even he didn't know where to find them, so it really wouldn't help me to request directions to that one.

"I like the hearts one the best," Goldie whispered in my ear. "Pick that one."

I brushed her off like a buzzing insect. "I'll pick whichever one I please, thank you."

"Well?" said the dwarf. "Which is it?"

I took a breath. "The Wine Well," I said. "Tell me where the well is."

The dwarf smiled his big, unnerving smile. "A fine choice." He pointed a stubby finger downstream. "Follow the stream until it becomes a river. When the river bends to the east, you go west and up the mountainside until you come to a large boulder shaped like a fish jumping out of the water. From the fish boulder, you travel north until you come to a graveyard."

"A graveyard!" Goldie shivered.

I didn't like it, either, but I wasn't about to say so. I tried to sound brave. "And is the well in the graveyard?"

"No," said the dwarf. "But in the graveyard, the trees whisper."

"Whisper?" I asked. "Are the trees full of nymphs?"

The dwarf seemed almost impressed. "A human who knows of tree nymphs!"

"We've been trying to catch one," said Goldie. "But it's very difficult."

"Yes," said the dwarf. "Slippery as a memory, those nymphs, but they will lead you the rest of the way."

"To the well?" I asked.

The dwarf nodded. "Tree nymphs are fond of the well and fond of sharing it with others."

I nodded. Perhaps the tree nymphs had been trying to lead me there all along. Maybe they themselves drank from The Wine Well and that's why their wings had curing powers. Now instead of catching a nymph, I could go directly to the source of power.

"Thank you, Dwarf," I said. "You've been very helpful. I hope to catch your beard again someday."

The dwarf scowled, his eyes dark as coal. "Drink deeply of the wine. Its effects are most beneficial." He hopped across the stream, leaping nimbly from stone to stone, and disappeared in the tall grass. A wicked little laugh trailed behind him.

"He wasn't at all pleasant," said Goldie. "Do you suppose all dwarves are like that?"

"Granny says so," I said, and walked quickly along the stream.

Goldie trotted to catch up with me. "Do you think we'll make it to the well before nightfall?"

"We? You weren't planning to come with me, were you?"

"Of course! You'll need a companion for your journey. You don't wish to be alone in The Woods. It's so spooky!"

As a matter of fact, that is precisely what I wished. "That's very kind of you, but—"

I stopped short and stared down at my feet. My path was gone. Goldie stood right next to me. No shock had steered her away. No wind had forced her off. I stomped my feet, trying to make my path reappear. It didn't. I turned around and walked back until it appeared again beneath my feet, stretching in the direction of home but not in the direction I wanted to travel.

"What's wrong?" Goldie asked. "Did you forget something?"

"No," I said. I'd never been in The Woods without my

path, not since that day with the bear. But what choice did I have? The well was in one direction, and Granny was in the other, alone, sick, dying. I heard her words echo inside me.

Don't be afraid.

I wasn't afraid. I wouldn't be. I took a breath and stepped off my path.

CHAPTER EIGHT
Your Heart's Desire

I walked as quickly as I could, with Goldie skipping boisterously beside me. Without my path, I felt exposed and vulnerable. My heart thrummed as fast as a rabbit's. I felt skittish as a rabbit, too, jumping at every noise and movement in The Woods.

Goldie's presence was like a swarm of mosquitoes. Every word she spoke, every little movement she made, was like an itchy bite, and her curls made me dizzy. They bounced more than grasshoppers. I wanted to take an ax and chop them all off. Or her head. That might be nice. But I bet even if I chopped off her head, she'd keep talking.

"Mummy named me Goldie so I would find lots of gold, of course, and for a while it really worked. It's like I could smell the gold between the rocks, and Mummy and Daddy were so proud of me. Now there's no gold in The

Mountain anymore, but I can sense other things that are golden, too, like yellow flowers and honey, and so I'm not completely worthless, though some people think so." She sighed. I imagined she was thinking of the boy she wanted to give a love potion to.

Daylight faded quickly, and the air grew chill. If I had my path, I would continue on in the dark, but without it I could be attacked by bears, mountain lions, and wolves.

"We'd better stop for the night," I said. "It's getting dark."

"Oh, yes, of course," said Goldie, looking around. "Where will we stay? Is there an inn nearby? Do you suppose they'll have a supper? I'm quite hungry. And I wouldn't mind a soft bed."

"There's not an inn or village for miles, Goldie. We'll have to sleep in The Woods."

"Sleep in The Woods! You can't be serious!"

I shook my head. "You're welcome to go back to the village. You can stay in any of the houses there. I'm sure no one will mind."

Goldie tugged anxiously at her curls and glanced back the way we had come. I half expected her to turn around and march straight home, but she didn't.

"Well, I suppose every quest has its risks," she said, and went to work, humming as she scooped leaves for her bed. I sighed and gathered leaves and pine needles for my own bed.

It was a long, restless night. Goldie chattered endlessly, telling me all about her mummy and whatnot, and when she finally fell asleep, she snored like a bear in a cave. I tossed and turned, and just when I was on the brink of sleep, a wolf howled.

Come, he said. He was calling for his pack, but he never got an answer.

The next morning I awoke to the most horrid cheerfulness.

"Wake up, Red! It's a glorious morning!"

It took me a moment to remember where I was and who was with me. I was in The Woods with Goldie, and I'd had the worst night's sleep of my life.

"Leave me alone," I grumbled, and pulled my cloak over my head.

"But it's so sunshiny and pretty! And I picked you some flowers. Here, smell them."

Goldie shoved something beneath my cloak, and my nose was accosted by a bunch of blossoms and their overwhelming perfume. "Get away—*aaaahaaaaCHOO!*"

"Oh, dear, I'm sorry. Let me help you." Goldie reached down to pick me up. I tried to slip under her arm, but my hair got tangled in one of her buttons.

"Aaaargh!"

"Oh! I'm sorry! I got it." Goldie yanked on my hair.

"Grrrrrr!"

"Hold still!"

"You hold still!" We wrestled and I growled until I finally ripped myself free, and we both tumbled back at the very moment an arrow hit the ground right between us.

Horst tore through the brush, his bow nocked with an arrow. "Ha! I got you, you wily . . . girls?"

Goldie and I sat frozen on the ground.

"Where's the wolf?" Horst swatted at the trees and brush, surely frightening every creature within a mile.

"There's no wolf," I said. "Only us."

"Shhhhh. I heard him growling just now."

"That was Red," said Goldie.

"Who's Red?"

"Her." Goldie pointed at me.

"That's a girl. Not a wolf."

"She's a very growly girl."

Horst huffed in frustration. "Well, what are you doing all the way out here growling like a wolf?"

"We're on a quest!" said Goldie.

"A quest?" Horst asked. "What kind of quest?"

"To save Red's granny!"

"The witch? What's wrong with her?"

"She's dying, so we're going to find—"

"Ingredients," I cut Goldie off. "We're gathering ingredients. For medicine." I sent Goldie a sharp look. I didn't think it wise to make our true quest widely known.

Horst nodded, a look of pity in his eyes. "Death is a terrible thing. Terrible."

"It's only a cold," I said.

"Well, a cold can kill an old person," he said gruffly. "And even if they do get better, everyone dies eventually, don't they?"

I flinched, feeling the sting of his words.

"Excuse me," said Horst. "That was rude, wasn't it?

Don't pay any attention to old Horst. I'll tell you what. You help me, I'll help you."

"How?" I asked.

"Old Horst knows a thing or two about staying alive. I've survived more than colds." He laughed a wheezy laugh. He wasn't exactly the picture of health, and I doubted he knew as much as Granny or dwarves about staying alive, no matter his age, but I thought it would be impolite to say so.

"What do you want from me?"

"You seen a wolf in these parts? Big black beast?"

"Sometimes," I said.

"I've been tracking him for months, but he's slippery as a ghost, always evading me. If you help me catch the wolf, I might be able to help your granny with that cold of hers. Horst knows a thing or two, yes?"

Horst hobbled over and plucked his arrow from the ground. As he bent down, I noticed a pouch dangling around his neck. It was a leather pouch about the size of my fist. I wondered what was inside it. Gold? Gems? Teeth?

Horst straightened up, bones creaking in a dozen different places. "If you see the wolf, just—"

Something rustled in the bushes. Horst lifted his bow. A gopher darted out and skittered away. Horst shot and missed. He grumbled and hobbled over to retrieve his arrow again.

Poor Horst. He couldn't possibly last much longer.

"We'd better get going," I said. "Lots of ingredients to gather."

"Don't forget," said Horst, "if you see that wolf, you call for Horst!"

I nodded. "Come on, Goldie." I was anxious to be on our way.

"Goodbye, Mr. Huntsman!" Goldie waved.

As we drew farther away, I glanced over my shoulder. Horst was watching us through the trees.

We walked along the river for most of the morning. The river was straight for as far as I could see, and I was beginning to doubt the dwarf's directions. Had he misled me somehow? Tricked me? We walked for three miles, perhaps four. The terrain became rougher, and the trees grew thicker along the river, making it difficult to travel with any sort of speed. My legs grew sore and my energy waned quickly.

"I'm hungry," Goldie said at almost the exact moment I thought it. With Horst's surprise appearance, I had forgotten all about breakfast. "I wish I would have thought to bring some food on this journey. It's always a good idea."

"The Woods are full of food," I said. "We can find some berries." I searched through the trees and shrubs until I found a wild raspberry bush. Goldie and I ate right off the bush until our hands were stained with the juice.

"Now I'm thirsty," said Goldie.

"The Woods have water, too." We went to the riverbank and slurped the cold water from our hands.

"Let's rest a moment," I said. I unlaced my shoes,

peeled off my stockings, and dipped my feet in the water. I gasped at the shock of its icy coldness, but it felt good on my sore feet. I waded in a little farther, hiking up my skirt. The current tugged at my legs, but the surface was smooth as glass, so I could glimpse my own reflection staring back. My hair was a tangled mess and my face was smudged with dirt. I looked wild, like some creature of the trees. I saw another face, too, one quite different from my own. I whirled around to see who stood behind me, but no one was there except Goldie.

"What is it?" she asked, noticing my alarm.

I looked back. The face was still there. It was that of a woman, ethereally beautiful, with pale blue eyes and hair like gossamer. Her skin was ghostly white, and her ears were pointed.

This was no reflection. It was a water sprite.

I stumbled back, splashing wildly, and scrambled onto the bank.

"What's wrong?" asked Goldie.

"There's a sprite," I warned.

"Sprites!" said Goldie. "Where?" She leaned over the water, but I tugged her back.

"Don't go near it!"

The sprite rose from the water like a ghost from its grave. She floated forward, her sparkling fins swirling around her like a silken gown.

"Come," said the sprite. "I will give you your heart's desire." Her voice was rich, a dark liquid, sweet as molasses spreading on my tongue.

Granny had told me about water sprites. They were

known for luring people in with false promises and be-
witching words, but the moment you touched them, they
would drag you beneath the water and feed on all your
wishes, sucking out your very soul.

The sprite stretched forth a hand, slender and webbed
between the fingers. She looked so delicate, so harmless.
Her beauty was captivating.

"What do you wish?" she said. "I can give you all that
you desire and more." She reached her hand toward me. I
stepped closer. All that I wished. Could she save Granny?
Our fingers were almost touching. The sprite smiled,
showing mossy teeth.

I pulled my hand back. No. She could not save Granny,
nor me. I knew better.

But Goldie did not. She was at the river's edge now
with another sprite.

The sprite spoke to her and Goldie reached out her
hand.

"Goldie, no!" I grabbed her by her curls and yanked
her back so we both fell on the muddy bank. More sprites
rose out of the water, reaching for us with webbed hands.

"Take my hand!"

"Don't be afraid!"

"We'll give you all that you wish!"

"Go away!" I shouted, tugging Goldie farther away
from the river and into the trees.

"Ouch!" she cried. "What are you doing? She said she
would give me anything I want!"

"It's a lie."

"But—"

"Don't ever go near the sprites," I scolded. "If you touch them, they'll drag you to the bottom of the river."

"How do you know?" Goldie asked.

"Because my granny said so."

"How does your granny know? Because she's The Witch of The Woods?"

I ignored her question. "Let's just keep walking. We're wasting daylight."

But Goldie was persistent. She was like a pecking hen. "I'll bet your granny knows a lot about magic, doesn't she?"

"A fair amount," I said.

"And I'll bet she taught you, right? Can you do lots of spells and make potions and things?"

"No," I said, and walked a little faster. "I don't do magic."

"Why not? If I knew how to do magic, I'd use it all the time!"

"You think that until you make a mess of it. Magic can cause all kinds of problems."

"You told me that before. Give me a real example. Not just something you made up. Something that really happened."

I sighed and rubbed my temples. I felt a sudden headache. "I nearly killed Granny once," I said. "A long time ago, I was performing a spell and I made a tree fall down on Granny and she almost died."

"Oh," said Goldie, and I thought that was the end of it, but then she said, "Maybe you just need some practice. Mummy said I fell down a lot when I was learning to walk. I got cuts and bruises, and I even knocked out my front teeth when I tripped over a bucket and smacked my mouth on the fireplace."

"What does that have to do with anything?"

"I kept walking, even though I sometimes got hurt. I kept trying until I got better and stopped getting hurt."

"But that's different," I said. "Walking is the simplest thing in the world."

"It's simple now, but it wasn't always. Some mistakes need to be made. Sometimes we have to fall down before we can stand up."

She said this all with an air of great wisdom that had the effect of annoying me greatly. "If you had almost killed someone by walking, would you still get up?"

Goldie folded her arms and gave me a disapproving look, as though she were my mother. "If magic is so dangerous, why are you trying to find magic now to save your granny?"

"That's different."

"How?"

"It's not *my* magic. I'm searching for magic that someone else made that will make Granny better."

"So not all magic is bad?"

"No, but that doesn't—"

"So why are you telling me I shouldn't look for a love potion? It's no different than what you're doing. You're just afraid, same as me."

"I am not afraid," I said, and I felt my temper rising. The heat inside me was bubbling up, ready to boil over.

"And I don't want to talk about this anymore." I walked a little faster.

"I was only trying to help," said Goldie, running to catch up.

"Stick to walking. You've had more practice." I walked even faster.

"You're rude!" Goldie shouted.

"And you're nosy."

"You're bossy."

I couldn't take this one more second. I spun around and roared in Goldie's face, "Yes, I am bossy! Now stop following me!"

Goldie winced as though she'd been stung. "I'm sorry, what did you say?"

"I'm going on my own from here. You should go home before it gets dark."

"But . . . I can help you. Don't you want help? I've always been very helpful, even Mummy says so."

I gritted my teeth and balled my hands into fists. If I opened them, I was certain streams of fire would shoot out of my palms. "The only way you could possibly help is by *going away*."

Goldie sniffed. Then tears spilled down her cheeks and she took off at a run. I could hear her wailing for a good long minute before it finally faded.

CHAPTER NINE

Wolf in The Woods

Good riddance! Goldie was gone, and at last I was alone. Just the way I preferred it. Finally I could hear myself think.

A cricket hopped across my feet, chirping loudly.

Harsh! Harsh! Harsh!

"Well, how else was I supposed to get rid of her?" I retorted. "She was driving me nuts!"

Harsh! Harsh! Harsh!

"Oh, go away. Now *you're* driving me nuts." The cricket hopped away, still chirping his chastisements.

Why should I feel guilty for dismissing Goldie? I hadn't invited her in the first place, and she had been slowing me down. It was already afternoon.

I ran for a bit to make up ground, enjoying the cool breeze and the sounds of birds and squirrels.

Rude! a squirrel squeaked at another for pulling her tail.

Bossy! chirped a bird to his mate as she ordered him about.

"Oh, be quiet!" I barked.

The sun sank behind the mountains as I walked on, casting the river and trees in shadow. I instantly started to shiver. That's when I realized I didn't have my cloak. I must have left it by the campsite. I couldn't very well go back and get it.

It got darker and colder. The thought of Goldie made me shiver again. I hoped she would get home all right, but what if she didn't? What if she ran into a wolf or bear or mountain lion?

The moon rose, revealing the river turned inky black and shadowy trees swaying in the breeze. I wrapped my arms tight around myself. It was considerably colder than last night. I needed warmth. I needed a fire.

I gathered some sticks, dry leaves, and pine boughs. I piled them all up and then struck two stones together, trying to make a spark, but none came. I hit the stones against each other again and again until I got so frustrated I hurled them. A few mice squeaked and skittered away. They thought the stones were owls coming to eat them. *I* could eat the mice. I was hungry enough.

And so cold. If I couldn't make a fire, I might freeze to death. I certainly wouldn't be able to sleep.

Goldie's words needled me.

You're just afraid.

Pfffft! I was never afraid. Fire was magic at which I

excelled. I concentrated all my energy on the pile of sticks and leaves and snapped my fingers. I felt the magic sputter inside me. A slight breeze rushed over my little pile, but no fire came. Not even a spark. Of course. The one time I actually *wanted* to start a fire, only the wind blew. Less than an hour ago, I had felt I could spew fire out of my nostrils.

I tried it again. I snapped my fingers and flicked out my hands to make the magic come. This time a bigger wind came. It rushed through the trees and scattered my sticks and leaves. Even the clouds shifted overhead, covering the moon. Had *I* done that?

I gave up on the fire. With my luck, I would probably set myself on fire or blow myself away in the wind. That wouldn't do Granny any good.

I piled up the leaves and sticks again and then nestled myself inside them. I hugged my knees to my chest. The wind whistled through the trees. The clouds blackened, and a drop of rain splashed on my nose, then another and another, until the sky tore open and emptied its contents. I was soaked in seconds. I crawled on my hands and knees beneath a pine tree and curled my knees to my chest. The rain pounded, the wind rushed, and the thunder rumbled.

I shivered violently. So cold. I hoped Goldie had gotten home all right. I wished I hadn't yelled at her. I wished I wasn't alone.

I *wasn't* alone.

Something was near. I couldn't see it, but I sensed it, the powerful presence of a wild beast. I sat up and scanned the black trees.

I saw his eyes first, a soft green glow that lit the black

shape of him. The wolf moved slowly and silently through the trees, eyes locked on me. It was like he had followed me all this time, watching me become weak and helpless so he could attack. Well, I might be lost and cold and hungry, but I wasn't weak or helpless. I grabbed a stick and stood up.

"Hey!" I shouted.

The wolf stopped mid-stride. Lightning flashed, and I saw that he was carrying something in his jaws—a rabbit or weasel, perhaps. Clearly he had already caught his supper, but that hadn't stopped him with Granny's pigs. Maybe he was after a second helping.

I raised the stick. "Get! Go away, you monster!" He took another step toward me. I threw the stick.

The wolf dropped whatever he was holding and dashed away.

I bent down to inspect it. It wasn't a rabbit, or any animal at all.

It was my red cloak.

I picked it up and flung it around my shoulders, throwing the hood over my head. I was instantly warmed down to my toes. Oh, glorious cloak!

The wolf may have saved my life. And I had been so harsh. I called him a monster.

Who was the monster here?

Far away, the wolf gave a high, lonesome howl.

Come! he called. His howl made him sound lonely and afraid, like a small child lost in The Woods.

I shuddered. I wasn't cold anymore, but the mournful cry rushed through me like a cold wind.

Come!

The wolf howled for a long time. No other wolves responded, but I listened until I fell asleep.

I woke the next morning stiff and hungry, my mouth dry as ash, but at least I had been warm through the night. I sat up and the red cloak slid off me, pricking my memory of the night before. I glanced around, searching for the wolf. I was still confused as to why he had helped me, but grateful nonetheless. It would have been a cold, restless night without the cloak.

I walked to the riverbank and checked for sprites. Seeing none, I bent down and drank until my belly was full, but I was still hungry. A red-breasted robin hopped toward the bank and pulled a worm out of the ground. A deer and her fawn grazed contentedly on some grass. Everyone was having breakfast except me. I filled my pockets with what berries I could find and ate as I walked. No time to waste.

The river seemed to flow in a straight line forever, but it was a beautiful morning. I tilted my head to the buttery sunshine. The hills in the distance rose like mounds of green salad, and the rocky cliffs along the river were like torn chunks of brown bread. Oh, I was just so hungry!

Something splashed in the water behind me, and I jumped back, clutching a tree, but it wasn't a sprite. It was the wolf, leg-deep in the river. I relaxed slightly. He dipped his head beneath the water, and when he came back up, he had a fat fish in his mouth. He flung it onto the riverbank, then dunked back in and had another fish in seconds.

The wolf picked up both fish with his jaws and then padded over to me. I stepped back a little. The wolf slowed. He dropped a fish just a few feet in front of me and dipped his head, inviting me to take it.

"For me?" I asked.

He barked.

Eat, he said, and nudged the fish toward me with his nose.

His eyes were so bright and keen. Again, I sensed greater intelligence behind his words, and my own magic wasn't enough to fully understand him.

I vaguely remembered an animal charm Granny had taught me when I was little, maybe five or six. Before the accident. She had seen that I loved the animals in The Woods, and I already had a natural ability to understand them, wild girl that I was.

Animal Charm
Squeak or growl, fur or feather
Beast and human come together
Tree or sky, lake or land
Flesh to fur, paw to hand

"Everyone has a particular animal they bond best to," Granny had told me. "When you find the right one, you'll feel it, and this charm will connect you in a more powerful way. You'll be able to hear their thoughts—even feel their energy and emotions. I was always partial to birds, but I'm not sure that's quite your animal. . . ."

No, of course not. Anyone named Red would be drawn to something much more vicious and wild.

I felt a tugging inside me, to move closer, to touch the wolf, but I stepped on a stick that snapped and the wolf bolted away. Well, I would enjoy the fish anyway. In the wolf's honor, I ate it raw. It was delicious.

My hunger satisfied, I continued on my journey with new vigor. I skipped stones in the river, and the fish jumped. The birds trilled, and I whistled with them. A woodpecker pecked in the distance, keeping rhythm with our song.

A bee landed on my shoulder, then another bee buzzed in my ear. A few steps farther, and suddenly there were bees everywhere. *What I wouldn't give for some honey right now.*

I followed the sound of buzzing down a gentle slope and then up a rocky hillside with caves and little crevices, perfect for a beehive. The bees swarmed around a narrow crevice. I approached them slowly until I saw the opening of the hive. My cloak was almost entirely covered with bees now, and I could practically taste the honey.

And then a deep growl echoed from one of the caves. I froze.

The growl came again. A big brown bear, five times my size, emerged from the cave. She was warning me to leave. I had trespassed on her territory, and she felt threatened. Bears are most dangerous when they feel threatened. I backed away from the hive, slowly, so as not to spook the bees. As soon as I was far enough away, I turned to run.

And came face to face with another bear. A small one.

The big bear lumbered toward me. She rose on her hind legs and roared, slashing her claws through the air.

My cub! Get away!

The horror of the situation dawned on me. I was standing between a mama bear and her cub.

CHAPTER TEN

Goldie's Wishes

Protection Spell
When faced with danger, have no fear
Take heaps of courage, a pinch of cheer

What a worthless spell! Who could possibly face this kind of danger with no fear? My whole body was flooded with fear. It was seeping from my pores, and the bear could probably smell it like bacon-wrapped pork chops.

She roared, showing fangs as long as my fingers.

Mine, she was saying.

"I'm going away now," I said. "You needn't be upset."

But the bear was already too upset to listen. Just because I can communicate with animals doesn't mean they won't rip out my throat.

The bear lunged, swiping her claws at me. I raised my arm as the claws raked down my cloak, shoving me to the ground. One claw grazed the top of my cheek. Soon my name and destiny would be fulfilled. Red as blood.

I closed my eyes.

The end.

"Here, bear!" said a voice. Not my own. The bear grunted and turned. I squinted to see. Directly behind the bear was none other than Goldie. She was standing right in the swarm of bees, her hands full of dripping honeycomb.

"Here, bear, come get some honey!" she coaxed like she was talking to a puppy.

The bear grunted again but got down on all fours and lumbered toward Goldie. She backed away, waving the honeycomb, then threw it into the bear's cave. The bear ambled to it, snuffling hungrily.

Goldie ran to me.

"How did you—"

"No time! Hurry, before the bear comes back!" She helped me to my feet, and we ran together, this time from a real bear, and I had the slightest twinge of guilt for the time I made Goldie think a bear was chasing her in The Woods when we first met. Real bears are quite a bit more terrifying than imaginary ones. We ran and ran until we were both out of breath, and then we collapsed against a tree.

"Great gourds!" said Goldie. "I thought you were going to be bear breakfast for certain!"

Goldie was a mess. Her curls were a ratty tangle, her dress was torn and smudged with dirt, and her face was covered in red welts. She had them on her hands, too, under all the sticky honey.

"Goldie," I said, "you're covered in bee stings."

"I'm all right," said Goldie, but I could tell by her swollen grimace that she wasn't. Luckily, I knew a quick remedy for burns and stings. It was one of the first potions Granny taught me. It had only one ingredient, and I always carried it with me.

Soothing Salve

Witch spit

I spat on Goldie's face several times.

"Ooh, gross! What are you doing? Is this how you thank people for saving you from certain death?"

"Rub it in," I said. "It will help the pain."

Goldie wiped her face, looking disgusted, but then I could tell it was helping. The swelling was going down, and her whole face relaxed.

"Spit on my hands," she begged.

"But you didn't say 'please,'" I said in a teasing voice.

"Red!" she scolded.

I spat on each hand five times, once for each swollen finger. Goldie rubbed her hands together and sighed.

"How did you find me?" I asked.

"I didn't," said Goldie. "I found the honey hive. Is this one yours, too?"

"No," I said.

"I thought not. I still couldn't get the honey with all the bees swarming, and then the bear came, so I hid, and then *you* came, and I just knew that bear was going to eat you, so I thought, I have to get some honey, because bears like honey, of course! So I held my breath and braved the swarm and got the honey, and so you're alive!"

"Goldie, you fool! You could have died from so many bee stings." Goldie's smile faltered. I bit my tongue.

Rude, ungrateful Red! Is that any way to thank someone for saving your life? By criticizing them? "But thank you," I said. "That was very brave, and if you hadn't nearly gotten stung to death, I'd surely be dead."

She looked down and blushed, then gasped. "You're bleeding!"

I lifted my hand. Blood trickled over my fingers. On my forearm, there was a gash about three inches long. I had forgotten that the bear had clawed me. I hadn't even felt the pain until now, but with the excitement wearing off, the sting was setting in.

"Do you want me to spit on it?" said Goldie.

"No thank you," I said. "It doesn't help with cuts, only burns and stings." I pressed my cloak over the wound to stop the bleeding.

"Well, at least your cloak isn't destroyed. It suits you so well."

I inspected my cloak. There wasn't a single tear, not a thread out of place. It was completely whole. But how? I had distinctly felt the bear's claws raking down my shoulder. Surely they should have ripped the fabric.

"Well, I suppose I should be on my way," said Goldie, twiddling her fingers.

"What way is that?" I asked.

"I'm not sure exactly. I was still hoping to find another dwarf, see if he could help me get a love potion? But I don't know which direction. . . ."

Oh, bother, I'd forgotten about the love potion. "Goldie, I really think you should forget the love potion. Do you really want to *make* a boy love you? Even if it works, it won't be real. Love isn't love unless he *chooses* to love you, right?"

Goldie's eyes went wide. Her chin trembled. "I don't need the love potion for a boy. I need it for my mummy!"

"Your mummy?"

She nodded. Her eyes brimmed with tears. "Now that there's no more gold in The Mountain, there's nothing special about me, and Mummy doesn't love me anymore." The tears came pouring out, running in rivers down her cheeks.

I opened my mouth and closed it again. This was not what I had expected. Perhaps my mother thought me a little odd. She might not understand me like Granny did, but I never questioned that she loved me. All mothers love their children, don't they?

Goldie turned and ran aimlessly through the trees. I could have let her go. I could have gone my own way, like I'd wanted to do from the start. But I couldn't just abandon her. And I couldn't really blame Goldie for wanting magic to get back someone she loved. Isn't that what I wanted, too?

I sighed. "Goldie, wait!"

I found her sprawled facedown in the dirt, sobbing. Soon she'd create her own swamp.

"I'm sorry I sent you away before," I said.

Goldie stopped crying, but she didn't get up.

I took a deep breath, steeling myself for what I was about to say. "You can still come with me. If you want. Of course, you probably don't . . ."

Goldie lifted her face off the ground. She had dirt smeared all over her, and her eyes were red and puffy, but they were hopeful. "Do you mean it?"

I nodded, and I realized that I did mean it. Even though she talked a lot and her bouncy golden curls made me dizzy, Goldie was slowly growing on me. And after last night, I really didn't want to be alone. "But you have to keep up," I said. "No dillydallying."

"Okay," said Goldie. She got up, brushed herself off, and wiped her tears, smearing more dirt across her nose and cheeks.

"Are you still looking for the well?"

"Yes," I said.

"Perhaps it could help me with Mummy, too. Do you think it could?"

"I don't see how it could, but who knows? We could find something else along the way."

"Right," said Goldie. "Then we haven't a moment to lose. We must find love and life or die trying!" She marched away with long, purposeful strides.

"This way, Goldie," I said.

"Oh. Yes, of course." She whipped around, and we continued along the river.

CHAPTER ELEVEN

A Bend in the River

"I didn't ever think we'd be friends," said Goldie, hopping from a log to a stone. Then she darted to a patch of buttercups and picked a handful.

"I didn't, either," I said. Our reunion seemed to renew Goldie's boisterous energy, making her as dizzying and annoying as ever, but I took it all in stride. Goldie said we were friends. No one except Rump had ever called me that, and I found it gave me a sort of warm, sweet feeling inside.

"Everyone told me to stay away from you, because of your name." She twirled a buttercup between her fingers. "And also because they said you're a witch, of course, but I think that just goes to show they didn't really know you. You're a little scary at first, but that's mostly because you frown a lot."

"I frown a lot?"

"Yes, you're frowning now." Goldie spun around me, then skipped ahead of me. She was like a hummingbird. She darted this way and that, taking twenty steps for every one of mine, and prattling a hundred words for each of mine. She was a girl who magnified and multiplied everything, and yet it had the backward effect of exhausting me while energizing her.

"I'm hungry," said Goldie. "Do you have any food?"

"Catch!" I tossed a few of the berries from my apron pocket, and they all bounced off her face. "Almost. Try again." I threw just one berry, and Goldie caught it in her mouth. I rewarded her with a handful, which she promptly devoured.

"Do you think you can sense red things like I sense golden things?" she asked, juice running down her mouth.

"Maybe," I said. I had never really thought about this, but it seemed reasonable. I did find a lot of wild raspberries and strawberries and plums, but I always assumed they were simply plentiful in The Woods and easy to find and it had little to do with destiny. Destiny wasn't something I was so certain about anyway. I knew names were powerful, and sometimes things happened that we had no control over, but I disliked the idea that I couldn't determine my own future. I wanted to decide for myself how things would go for me. I supposed that was why I was here now, searching for a magic well, because destiny had delivered bad news. I was going to give destiny a good punch in the face.

"I'm still hungry," said Goldie when the berries were gone. "Maybe we can catch some fish." She started toward the water.

"Don't be stupid," I said. "Don't you remember the sprites?"

Goldie scowled. "I remember the sprites. I just thought maybe some fish would be nice."

I looked away, remorse needling me. "I'm sorry," I said. "I just thought you might have forgotten."

"Well, I didn't," she said. "I never forget anything." She lifted her chin and walked faster. So I walked faster, too, and then she went faster, so I went faster, and then Goldie ran, so I ran, too. We raced down the river. I pulled ahead of Goldie, and I was pretty proud of myself until—

Schleeeoop!

I sank into the ground up to my knees. Goldie stopped just short of the mud puddle. "Golly glops! What a mess!" She plugged her nose.

It smelled like goat dung, and it looked like it, too, sort of a brownish green with streaks of yellow. A toad croaked and hopped away. I had clearly invaded her home. Well, I had no objection to leaving. I pulled my legs up, but one shoe stayed in the mud. I had to dig down to get it out. It came loose with a great squelchy slurp and splattered mud all over my face.

Goldie stifled a laugh. So I grabbed a handful of mud and flung it at her face. She stopped laughing. I chuckled and pulled myself free of the bog, then a glob of mud smacked me in the back of the head. I felt the muck dripping down my hair. I turned around to Goldie. She was brushing off her hands with a satisfied smirk.

"You know what this means, don't you?" I said.

"What?" Goldie shifted nervously.

"War!" I flung two handfuls of mud. She shrieked and stumbled forward into the muck, but as soon as she came back up, she lobbed an apronful of mud in my face. I gagged and sputtered.

"You have a little something on your face," said Goldie.

"That's funny, you have a little something everywhere." I lunged at Goldie and tackled her into the mud. We rolled this way and that while the mud squished and squelched with such a range of pitches it was nearly musical. The smell was vile, but it didn't keep us from smearing the mud in each other's faces, laughing so hard we couldn't stop.

"Look!" said Goldie. "A bend in the river!"

She was right! The river was bending to the left, which was probably what had formed this bog in the first place. We slogged our way out of the mud, soggy and smelly as rotting fish guts, but neither of us minded. I didn't think I'd laughed quite like that since . . . since the last time I had a friend, when Rump still lived on The Mountain.

Goldie put her muddy arm through mine, and we walked away from the river, our footsteps squelching in a cheerful rhythm.

By early afternoon, we found the rock shaped like a fish. Its curved body was poised as though jumping out of water, just as the dwarf had said.

"Now which way?" asked Goldie.

"The dwarf said north. And we were going west, I

think, so . . ." I tried to get my bearings, but I wasn't at all certain until something whispered in my ear. A yellow leaf drifted past me, floating along an invisible path.

"Follow the nymph!" I said. We walked around a narrow ledge on the mountainside that gave way to a steep, rocky hillside and finally smoothed to thick woods dotted with stones. Gravestones.

We instantly slowed, suddenly wary of what lay ahead.

The graveyard looked ancient. Some of the stones were crumbling, covered in lichen, and the names etched in them were nearly unreadable from so many years of rain and wind and snow. I couldn't help but study the names as I passed.

AGATHA. BELINDA. JACOB. BERNARD.

My skin prickled as I read. People who had once been alive were now dead and buried in the ground, nothing but bones and dirt. No matter how rich or poor, how powerful or helpless, they all died.

"I don't like graveyards," said Goldie.

"There's nothing to be afraid of," I said, though my own voice trembled.

"What if we see a ghost?"

"Then we must hope it is a friendly one."

BERTHA. HUGO. KLAUS.

The trees began to whisper.

"Do you hear that?" Goldie asked.

"Shhhh." The whispering grew louder, like a wind rustling the leaves, except I felt no breeze.

"It's a ghost!" whimpered Goldie.

"It's not a ghost," I said. "It's the tree nymphs." They seemed excited, or at least they were louder than I'd ever heard them before. Granny said when people die, the tree nymphs soak up all their memories and whisper their ancient secrets and wisdom to those who will listen.

I walked between the gravestones, tilting my ears toward the trees.

ROSAMUNDE. SIEGMUND. GUIDO.

I could almost hear the nymphs saying the names aloud with their tiny clicks and whispers. Then the nymphs took flight, all the leaves rising off the branches at once. They swirled around us, hundreds of them, maybe thousands. Surely I could catch at least one.

I jumped and clapped my hands over the nymphs. I tried to use my cloak as a net, but the nymphs evaded me at every turn. Then they swarmed all around me, tugging on my cloak and hair. They did the same to Goldie, pulling us each farther into the graveyard, where more tree nymphs rose off their branches. Finally they all swirled up into the sky in a funnel, leaving all the surrounding trees as bare and lifeless as the graveyard. But beyond the trees lay the treasure we were seeking.

A well.

CHAPTER TWELVE

Well, Wine, and Witch

The well didn't look magical. It was overgrown with weeds and thistles, and the stones were cracked and crumbling.

"Do you think this is the right well?" Goldie asked.

I was doubtful, except we had followed the dwarf's directions so exactly, and everything had matched his description.

"There's only one way to be certain," I said.

I walked to the well and leaned over the edge. The bottom was black as a cave at midnight, and I couldn't smell anything at all. I turned the rusty stile so the bucket lowered down. There was a *plish*. I heaved the bucket up and looked inside. Goldie gasped.

"It's wine, Red! Red wine!"

The nymphs swirled over the roof of the well,

whispering excitedly. This had to be The Wine Well. I felt that tingly feeling I get when there's magic around—surely this would restore Granny's magic, her life, her youth. . . .

"Do you think we should drink some?" asked Goldie.

"The dwarf said it would restore youth," I said. "We're already young. I just need to bring some back to Granny."

"How will you carry it?" Goldie asked.

I hadn't considered that. I had nothing in which to carry the wine, but then there was another rush and swirl of nymphs, and what I'd assumed was a nearby grove of trees was revealed to be a house, or at least what was left of one.

It was a large manor, most certainly abandoned. The shutters were chipped and hanging off their hinges, dead ivy climbed the walls and frame, and the stone chimney was only half standing.

"It doesn't seem like anyone lives there," said Goldie.

"No," I said.

"But perhaps there might be a bottle or a jug inside."

"Yes," I said, though neither of us moved. A few nymphs settled on the roof of the dilapidated house, making it look all the more overgrown and haunted.

"You go first," said Goldie.

I walked slowly to the door. It was cracked and chipped. The knob and hinges were orange with rust.

"I think we should knock," said Goldie. "It's the polite thing to do."

"Yes, of course," I said. "We can't go barging into other people's houses."

I gave a quick rap on the door. There was no answer. I knocked again, and the door fell inward. Clouds of dust billowed up as it crashed to the floor.

I covered my mouth with my cloak as the dust settled. "I don't think anyone's home," I said.

"Except maybe ghosts," said Goldie.

We walked slowly inside and the floorboards creaked beneath our feet. It must have been a grand house once. It looked as though it had been abandoned centuries ago. Everything was covered in thick layers of dust from floor to ceiling. Walls, nooks, and candlesticks were festooned with cobwebs, and the drapes and tapestries had been eaten away by moths.

A dining table was set for two with fine china and silver and crystal goblets, as though the inhabitants had just sat down to a special supper and then—poof!—disappeared, leaving their meal to rot and collect dust.

And there was a wine bottle, too. With a cork. I took the bottle off the table. It was empty. When I turned around, something rustled and hooted. I jumped back and Goldie screamed. An owl was perched on the edge of the fireplace. He turned his head and looked at us with one amber eye.

"Hello, owl," I said.

Hoo! Hoo! said the owl.

"What did he say?" Goldie asked.

"He said it's not polite to barge into other people's houses."

"Oh, is this his house, then?" Goldie asked.

Hoo-hoo-HOOT!

"No, he said owls aren't people."

"Oh, yes, of course. Well then, whose house is it?"

"Albert?" called a soft voice. "Is that you?"

Goldie and I both gasped as a figure emerged from a cobwebbed corner. It was a woman, thin and pale as mist. She was draped in dust and cobwebs like a forgotten figurine on a shelf. The only bit of color on her was her lips, glistening red.

Goldie clutched my arm. "It's a ghost!"

"A ghost?" said the woman. "No. They call me The Well Witch, whoever *they* are, though I don't prefer to be called a witch. It sounds old and ugly, and I am neither." It was difficult to tell how old she was. She had the air of something ancient, like old books, dusty and worn at the edges. Her skin was like yellowing paper, yet her voice was high and thin, almost childish. She could have been twenty or a hundred.

"Have you seen Albert?" she asked.

"Who's Albert?" I asked.

"My love. He should have been home for supper by now. He hasn't been well lately, you see, and I have the most delicious wine to revive his strength." In her hands she held a crystal goblet, empty but for a puddle of red at the bottom, just the color of her lips.

"Is that wine from the well?" I asked.

"Yes," said the woman. "It's the most delicious wine."

"I was told the wine can make you young again," I said.

"Yes, it does," said the woman. "When Albert grew old and took sick, I devoted all my powers to restoring youth and vitality."

"And it works?" I asked, feeling the hope fluttering madly in my stomach.

"Oh, yes, as you see, I'm quite young. I've been young forever." As she spoke, her face seemed to shift. It was subtle, but I thought her nose swelled a little and her lips thinned. Probably just the shadows.

"May I take some of your wine?"

The woman glided to the table and picked up another wineglass. "Follow me." She glided to the entrance and right over the fallen door, saying nothing about it.

In the sunlight, the woman looked older than before. She had some lines around her mouth, and her eyes had crow's-feet.

"I was old myself once," she said, her voice just a little raspier. "I can hardly remember anything from that old, old life, except that Albert was sick. He'll be well again once he has some wine. Where is he? He's always slipping away from me."

I looked around, wondering if Albert was as strange and dusty as this woman. She dipped her goblet into the bucket and brought forth the wine. "Anyone who drinks the wine will not die, but regain their youthful strength and beauty. I will gladly share it with you. I think everyone should have it."

"We don't need it," I said. "We're already young."

"Yes, of course. Someday, perhaps. Sooner than you imagine. Aging happens so quickly, it seems. One day you'll feel it creeping on your skin like spiders." As she said this, wrinkles appeared around her eyes, and the folds around her mouth deepened, as though an invisible sculptor were etching them into her face. "It's a terrible feeling to grow old." Her body sagged. Her shoulders hunched. "Old age, sickness, and death. They're curses. Eternal youth, that is the greatest power anyone can have, don't you agree?" Her breathing was raspy and labored. Brown spots appeared on her skin, and the veins darkened and rose on her hands.

Goldie nodded. "Of course. Of course we agree."

"Now I must drink. I can feel myself withering away." The woman—now an old crone—took a drink, long and deep, and as she did, the years seemed to melt away. The brown spots faded, her skin smoothed, and her shoulders straightened. The tree nymphs rushed all around, clicking and whispering excitedly as the woman drained the goblet, almost as though they were being revived as well. By the time she had emptied the goblet, the woman was young again.

"Great ghosts!" said Goldie. "That's incredible!"

The young woman started. "Oh! Where did you two come from?" She looked between us as though we had appeared out of thin air.

Goldie and I looked at each other, confused. "We've been here all along. We came for some of your wine. I wanted to take some to my granny. She's sick."

"Sick? Albert was sick. He should have been home by now. Have you seen him?"

"Not since we've been here." Something very odd had just happened. The hair at the nape of my neck prickled. "What's your name?" I asked. "You never told us."

"My name?" said the woman. "Why, they call me The

Well Witch, whoever *they* are, though I don't prefer to be called a witch. It sounds old and ugly, and I am neither."

"But what other name? What name were you born with?"

"Born with? I was never born. I've lived forever, you see, and so I have no name. Names are for mere mortals. Things that grow old and die. I do neither, because of my wine. It's quite delicious." She sipped more wine, and again time reversed itself. Her cheeks turned round and rosy, her waist slender, and she even shrank a few inches, so that she now looked to be fifteen or sixteen.

Goldie was transfixed. "Red, I think I know how to make Mummy love me again," she whispered, but before I could ask how, the woman noticed us and gave a start.

"Oh! Where did you two come from?"

The cold feeling set into ice as I realized exactly what had happened. The wine had made her young again, but it had also taken away her memories. It turned back time, but only for her, and the tree nymphs soaked up the memories as she lost them with each sip.

"We came for your wine!" Goldie said eagerly. "We want to have some."

"Of course," said the woman. "Everyone should have it." She held out the wine goblet and Goldie reached for it, but I yanked her back.

"Don't, Goldie!" I whispered. "That wine erased her memory. She doesn't even remember us."

"I know," Goldie whispered back. "But don't you see? If I drink some of this wine, then I'll be little again. Mummy adored me when I was little. She said I was the most precious thing in the world." She turned back to The Well Witch. "Can the wine make me younger than I am now?"

"Of course," said the woman, smiling. "Young and beautiful. That's why I made it. Old age and death are the greatest curse of this world. Now you can break the curse." She held the goblet out to Goldie.

Goldie wrapped her fingers around its stem. Was the wine really so bad? Maybe if I gave Granny just a sip, it wouldn't make her forget too much—just a few years. She'd still remember me, but she'd be well. She wouldn't die. But how much wine could I give her before she did forget me? That would almost be worse than death, for Granny to live and not know who I was.

Goldie lifted the goblet to her lips.

"Goldie, no!" I lunged and slapped the goblet away. It fell to the ground and broke in two. "Oh, what a pity," said the witch. "That was my best goblet."

I watched the wine seep into the ground, my heart pounding as shriveled weeds turned an unnatural green. "Come on, let's go." I grabbed Goldie's hand, but she pulled away and looked at me like I was a troll. "Who are you?"

I looked closely at Goldie's lips. They were red and glistening. A tree nymph was perched on her shoulder.

Curses. Goldie had swallowed some of the wine.

CHAPTER THIRTEEN

Missing Memories

Goldie turned to The Well Witch and squinted her eyes. "Mummy?"

"Am I?" said the witch. "I suppose I could be. I always wished for a daughter, though Albert wanted a son. Where is he? He should have been home by now. Have you seen my Albert?"

"No, and you're not her mummy. Come on, Goldie." I tried to grab her hand again, but she wrenched herself free.

"Don't touch me!" Goldie shrieked. "My mummy told me you're an evil witch and you do bad things."

How much time had been erased? Goldie looked exactly the same. She couldn't have swallowed more than a splash of wine, which I hoped meant only a tiny bit of her memory had been taken. Unfortunately, it was the bit that included our friendship. Still, I didn't understand why she was being so mean. She hadn't been this way when we'd first met. Had the wine changed her nature when it took away her memories? Did she really believe I was an evil witch?

"She's a witch, too," I said, pointing to The Well Witch. "She just gave you wine that made you forget we're friends."

"Ha!" said Goldie. "I'd never be friends with someone like you!"

"Oh, yes, the wine," said the witch. She dipped the other crystal goblet in the wine and held it out to us. "Here. Have some. It's very refreshing."

"Oh, thank you." Goldie reached for the wine again, but I yanked her back by her hair.

"No thank you," I said.

"Ouch, you mean girl! Let me go! Mummy!" She reached for the witch, who was drinking the wine again and growing younger still. Too young to be anyone's mummy.

"She's not your mummy," I said. "Come on." I dragged Goldie away from the well and into the graveyard while she pulled and thrashed and scratched.

"Let go of me! Just who do you think you are?" Finally Goldie wriggled free and ran off through the gravestones. She couldn't remember my quest to save Granny, and she clearly wanted nothing to do with me.

But she had no way of knowing where we were or how to get home. Even now, I could see she was confused, wandering aimlessly, with no path to guide her. She wouldn't last a day.

"Goldie, wait!" I ran to catch up with her.

"Go away," she grumbled.

"But I want to help you."

"I don't need help."

"Do you even know where you are?"

She glanced sideways at the gravestones and the whispering trees. "In The Woods, of course. And this is a graveyard, so I can't be far from the village."

Goldie continued walking, looking every which way, trying to decide which direction to go. I think she knew something strange had just happened, even if she didn't know what it was.

Granny said that memory charms are some of the trickiest magic, because you can't really erase someone's mind. You can only muddle it, like throwing dirt in clear water and swishing it around. I wondered if there was any way to make Goldie's memories clear again. Dirt settles eventually, right?

I followed a few steps behind Goldie. Every now and then, she looked back at me suspiciously, so I focused on the gravestones, reading the names again as we walked.

LEONARD. CHARLOTTE. HEINRICH.

Goldie walked a little faster.

WILHELM. OTTO . . .

I stopped, squinting at a particularly old gravestone. The stone was crumbling, but the name was clear.

Albert.

Oh, poor Albert. He wasn't going to make it home for supper after all, and The Well Witch would never see her love. She'd wait and wait and make herself young again and again, forgetting everything except Albert, and Albert would never come home.

I moved on, past the graveyard and the whispering trees. Away from The Wine Well and The Well Witch. Away from the magic to save Granny. I wondered if there could be a magic out there that would keep Granny with me without taking too much away.

Goldie walked maybe a hundred feet ahead of me, ambling in an aimless, haphazard way. She glanced back at me over her shoulder and—

Schleeeoop!

She sank knee-deep in the bog.

I laughed, remembering our mud fight, but then Goldie started crying, so I took her arm and tried to help her out.

"Don't touch me!" she screamed. "Stop following me! Stop it, or I'll . . . I'll hit you!" She raised her hand into a little fist that probably couldn't punch down dough. Still, she looked fierce. She breathed through clenched teeth, and her teary eyes were blazing for a fight.

It was a strange reversal, me chasing after Goldie, and

Goldie making threats and fists. But I wasn't about to let her go off on her own. I was Red, I reminded myself, and if nothing else, red was a stubborn color. I hadn't dragged Goldie all this way and gone through all this trouble just to have *her* ditch *me*.

I stomped both my feet in the bog. Mud splattered on Goldie's cheek. "You don't scare me," I said. "I'll come and go as I please."

She wiped her face. "Oh! You horrible girl! Didn't your mother teach you any manners at all?"

"No," I said. "But my granny taught me all sorts of spells and potions and curses. I'm very good at the curses."

Goldie scrambled out of the bog to dry ground. "Witch! Keep away from me! You're evil!" She spoke each word like she was cracking a whip. And it stung. Goldie had never been mean to me like this. Maybe that wine did something else besides take away her memories.

"Fine." I lifted my hands in surrender. "I'll keep my distance, but I can't help it if we're traveling in the same direction."

"Fine," said Goldie, and she stood and huffed along the riverbank.

"Keep your eyes open for bears and wolves!" I called. "I've seen quite a few around here."

She slowed her step and allowed me to walk just slightly closer. Now that I was chasing after her and she was trying to get me to leave, I couldn't help but feel a pinch of guilt for how I had acted before. I was getting a dose of my own medicine now.

As we traveled, the reality of my situation sank in. The

wine would not help Granny, or at least it didn't seem worth the consequences. What if she ended up forgetting me or, worse, hating me, as Goldie did now? I didn't know what to do. There were still two other options the dwarf had mentioned—The Red Roses and The Magic Hearts—but I didn't know where they were or how they worked. I had a feeling the dwarf had purposely kept those details vague to get me to choose the well. He'd probably hoped I'd drink the wine and forget about dwarves and how to make them tell me things. Little trickster.

The sun dipped behind the mountain peaks and the air grew chill. Bats burst from a cave high up on the mountainside, screeching for their supper.

"I'm stopping to make camp!" I called to Goldie. "You may continue without me if you wish. I won't follow you."

Goldie stopped and glanced back at me with suspicion. I went to work gathering wood and sticks to build a fire, then found a large pine with branches that arched to the ground to make a small shelter. Goldie moved to a tree a ways from me but close enough that we could see each other.

Once I had my fire going, I gathered some wild raspberries and edible roots. Goldie tried to do the same but had no success. I sat by the fire and ate a solitary meal. Usually I enjoyed the quiet of The Woods, but a quiet Goldie was disconcerting. It was like a songbird gone silent.

Goldie peeked out from her pine shelter, but when she saw me watching, she scrambled away.

"If you're cold, you can come closer to the fire," I said.

She didn't move for several minutes, but eventually she scooted closer, stopping a good five feet away. She wrapped her shawl tightly around her and shivered, then eyed my meal hungrily.

"I won't bite, you know," I said. "And you can have some berries. I promise they're not poisonous."

Hunger won out. She crawled toward me like a wary squirrel, snatched a handful of berries, and scrambled back. She devoured the berries in less than a minute. I finished my own meal and pretended not to notice Goldie inching toward the fire until she was only a couple feet away.

A few nymphs swirled around her head. She slapped at them with both hands.

"What *are* these things? They're making strange sounds."

"They're tree nymphs," I said. "I think they're trying to help you remember the things you forgot. Listen."

More nymphs swirled around Goldie, whispering and clicking. She continued to slap them away, then dropped her hands in defeat when it was clear they weren't going anywhere.

"What's the last thing you remember?" I asked.

"You yanked me by my hair away from that well!"

"No, before that. Yesterday. What happened yesterday?"

"Yesterday?" Goldie twisted her fingers in her mud-caked curls. "I was . . . arguing with Mummy. . . ."

"What were you arguing about?"

"She was very angry at me because I . . . I picked Gerhard's peaches and ate them without asking. They were so plump and golden, and I didn't think Gerhard would mind, but he was furious, and Mummy called me a little thief and said I had disappointed her. . . ." Goldie plopped down in the mud. Tears spilled down her cheeks.

I breathed a sigh of relief. She hadn't lost too much memory. Just a week, at most. She must have gotten only a splash of the wine on her tongue.

"I'm sure she forgives you," I said. "I'll bet she's looking for you now. I'll bet she's worried sick."

"No," said Goldie. "I don't think so." She continued to cry until she passed out from exhaustion. The nymphs swirled around her head, rustling and clicking. Perhaps they'd help restore her memories while she slept. I covered her with leaves to keep her warm, then nestled into my own bed.

But I couldn't sleep. The night was so *awake*. The moon was full and bright. It was like a crystal ball floating in the inky blue sky, magical and mysterious. The mountain peaks formed the silhouette of a giant palace, the trees their faithful sentinels, and the nighttime creatures the court musicians. An owl hooted, raccoons chattered, frogs croaked, and insects sang in a pulsing rhythm. It was a night Granny would have called enchanted, one so full of magic it could not be contained.

A wolf howled.

Come! he said.

I knew it wasn't just any wolf. It was *the* wolf. He howled again, closer this time.

Come! I could *feel* his words spark and rush inside me, tugging for me to answer.

The wolf came silently through the trees. I saw his glowing eyes first, and then the solid black outline of him, a shadow in the moonlight. I stood up; some wild impulse drove me to step toward him.

Was I a fool? The villagers always complained about wolves. They called them wild, vicious beasts, and when livestock went missing, a wolf was always to blame. But they never looked at the good side of wolves, how strong they were and how fiercely loyal to their pack. Wolves would never betray one of their own, but could I be one of its own?

The words of the animal charm formed on my lips.

> *Squeak or growl, fur or feather*
> *Beast and human come together*

Invisible threads tugged at me, drawing me to the wolf, beckoning me to come closer. I took a step toward him. The wolf stepped toward me. I got down on my hands and knees so our faces were level. The wolf lowered his head and stuck out a paw. I reached out a trembling hand.

> *Tree or sky, lake or land*
> *Flesh to fur, paw to hand*

Ever so gently, I brushed the tip of the wolf's paw, and the spark that connected us suddenly burst into flames. Fire surged through my veins, from my toes to my fingertips. Images flashed in my mind of wolves running wild through The Woods. I felt their energy, their strength. It rushed through my head like a powerful river current, sweeping me away so that I nearly lost myself.

Come, said the wolf. *Don't be afraid.*

CHAPTER FOURTEEN
Come

I stood slowly, like a colt trying to stand for the first time on spindly legs, and marveled at the wild power I felt inside of me. The wolf's voice was clearer than before, powerful and resonant, but it was more than that. I could *feel* his presence. I sensed his emotions, his instincts and movements. I placed my hand in his fur, and we walked, side by side, each of us sensing the other. It was like learning how to walk all over again. I stumbled with the feelings and images that rushed through me, but little by little they became familiar, and I found my balance. We started to run, just a shy trot at first, and then faster and faster, until I was certain my heart would burst, except it didn't. It just got bigger and stronger.

We raced through the trees, chased patches of starlight, and bounded in the glow of the full moon. We breathed in the endless sky, and all of it swirled together so that I felt small and big and everything all at once. I was the whole world and the whole world was within me.

We raced up the mountainside until we were on a cliff high above the river.

Home, he said, and I felt the familiar comfort of being at home. He led me around the cliffside to a cave opening. His den. I hesitated for just a moment, wondering if this was some kind of trap, but as the wolf moved, I felt myself pulled along by invisible strings, and my fears subsided.

I got down on my hands and knees to crawl through a tunnel until it opened up into a cavern. There was a small opening above that let in a sliver of moonlight. No one bigger than me could get in.

I half expected to find other wolves in the den, but it was empty. "Where is your pack?" I asked.

Gone. I saw a series of images, a strong pack of wolves, fierce and loyal, but one by one they disappeared. Hunted by a shadowy presence. Soon there was only one.

"You're alone," I said.

Wolf whined a little and pawed at the ground, and I felt an incredible sadness wash over me. Wolves were not meant to be alone. They thrived on the connection with their pack. Alone, this wolf was vulnerable and weak.

"How did they die?" I asked.

Monster, said the wolf. He tried to show me a vision, but it was dark and blurry—whatever this monster was, Wolf was clearly still afraid of it.

I placed my hand over the wolf's paw again. I felt a pulsing of energy.

Red, Wolf. Wolf, Red.

"Wolf," I said, as though I were pronouncing his name and destiny, like a newborn child's, which was silly. Animals don't have destinies like humans. Perhaps I was pronouncing it for myself—a part of my own destiny. "We are a pack now," I told him.

Pack, he said.

We left the den and stood on the edge of the cliff. Wolf tipped back his head and howled to the moon. I joined him, and our howls twined together like music, making the stars and moon tremble.

I hoped Granny could hear. She would recognize my voice, and it would make her feel alive, too.

I woke to an earth-shattering scream.

"Wolf! Run! There's a wolf!"

I sat up abruptly, and my head swam. Goldie was hightailing it up a pine tree, babbling nonsensically about a wolf.

Wolf . . .

I brushed Wolf's paw and remembered last night, howling at the moon. I had slept with my head in the crook of his stomach. It was soft and very warm.

Wolf yawned, showing sharp fangs and a long pink tongue.

"Run!" Goldie screamed from the tree. "That wolf's about to eat you alive!"

Eat, said the wolf, but I knew he wasn't thinking of

me, nor Goldie. He had fish on his mind, or rabbits or mice, or even berries. Any of those would do.

"It's all right, Goldie," I said. "He's not going to eat us."

"How do you know?" she called back.

"Because he's my friend."

"Only a witch would be friends with a wolf," said Goldie.

"You're right," I said. "I am a witch, but that doesn't make me evil."

"Mummy says it does," said Goldie.

"Have you ever considered that perhaps your mummy doesn't know everything? Now come down. I promise he won't hurt you."

"I don't have to do what you tell me," Goldie said.

"Fine," I grumbled. "Do whatever you want. Good luck finding breakfast. I'm sure you can chew on pine needles and slurp some sap." Goldie did not respond, nor did she come down from the tree. I was really starting to miss the old Goldie. This one was even grumpier than me! Also, her curls bounced less, and as much as they had annoyed me before, unbouncy curls are somewhat depressing. It almost made me want to try a cheering charm on her, but with my luck, she'd probably laugh herself to death. I'm sure I'd have a grand time trying to explain that to her mummy when she came searching.

I'm sorry, ma'am. Your daughter died of laughter. It's an infectious disease. I did everything I could.

Goldie would come down in her own sweet time, most likely when she smelled food. So I went in search of breakfast. Wolf padded alongside me. I placed my hands in the fur at his neck, marveling at our new connection, the energy pulsing through me, warm and wondrous. I wanted to run again, and Wolf, sensing my thoughts, immediately broke into a gallop.

We ran through the trees, in the morning mist, filling our lungs with cool air. Wolf saw a rise of hill, and images of wolves racing to the top rushed through me, so we raced to the top and then raced back down, and it was like being two creatures at once, or one creature in two places. We leapt over logs and drank in the fresh scent of pine and morning glory and . . . rabbit.

The smell slowed our steps, and we grew quiet, watching, listening. All my senses seemed heightened and right on the surface.

Something rustled in the brush just ahead of us. We circled it, Wolf on one side and me on the other. There was no need to speak. Wolf sent me an image of two wolves on opposite sides of a bush. One wolf pounced on the bush, and the other one caught the creature. I was to be the first wolf. That was the beauty of a pack. They worked together, seamlessly, cohesively. One.

I pounced on the bush.

The creature squeaked and hopped out the other side. Wolf leapt and caught a rabbit.

Breakfast.

On the way back to our camp, I gathered more berries.

I called up to Goldie in the pine tree, "We have breakfast!"

She didn't answer. Still ignoring me and afraid of

Wolf. Perhaps if she smelled breakfast, she'd come down. I went to work gathering wood and leaves to start a fire. I snapped my fingers to perform the drying spell. Nothing happened at first, but then a few tendrils of smoke rose up from the leaves, and a flame burst forth. I blew on it and added more sticks and leaves until I had a good fire going. I found two forked branches to make a spit. Wolf brought me the rabbit, and with a sharp rock I managed to skin it and get it roasting over the fire. I dusted off my hands, feeling quite satisfied with a job well done.

"Goldie, you're going to starve if you don't eat something. Come down."

Still no answer. Not even a sound. I moved closer to the tree. "Goldie?"

She wasn't there. I looked all around, by her bed of leaves, beneath the tree where I had slept, but saw no sign of her. Did she leave without me?

"Goldie?" I called. My heart was beating faster, panic rising in my chest. Horrible images of all the things that could happen to her raced through my mind. Bears. Mountain lions. Cliffs.

"Goldie!" I shouted.

Wolf brushed against my side, calming me. *Listen,* he said.

We held still and listened. I heard voices by the river. I hurried along the bank, straining to make out the words.

"Do you promise?" I heard Goldie say. I stepped through some heavy shrubs and found her. She was right at the edge of the bank, talking to someone.

"I promise," said a deep, soothing voice. "Anything you want."

My blood stopped cold in my veins. She was talking to a sprite. But she should know better. . . .

No! She didn't know better. Her memories of our previous encounter with sprites had been erased by the wine. She had no idea!

I ran toward her. "Goldie!" I shouted. "Get away!" She turned to me and frowned, then turned back to the sprite.

"I just want Mummy to love me," she said. "Can you make Mummy love me?"

"Yes, yes!" said the sprite, her words honey, molasses, and syrup. "All that you wish shall be yours. Come now!"

Goldie stepped into the water. She stretched her hand toward the sprite.

"Goldie, no! Don't touch her!" I shouted, but it was too late. Their fingers had touched. The sprite clasped Goldie in her webbed hands, and before Goldie could even utter a scream, she was dragged beneath the water.

CHAPTER FIFTEEN

Swimming with Sprites

The river rippled slightly and then flowed on like nothing had happened. The world was quiet, traitorously calm. Goldie had just been taken by a sprite! My mind raced for a rescue plan, but fear flooded all reason.

"Come with me," said another sprite, reaching for me. "Don't be afraid. What do you wish for?"

"I want my friend back, you monster!" I grabbed some rocks and threw them at the sprite, but she easily dodged them. I could still see Goldie struggling amidst a swirl of translucent fins, going deeper and deeper.

Without a thought, I dove in after her. The icy water shocked me, and then I was surrounded by sprites. "Take my hand!" they sang. "Anything you wish . . ."

I took a breath and plunged deeper.

The sprites swirled around, reaching for me, but they couldn't touch me unless I touched them first.

"Come with us!" they chanted. "We will give you your heart's desire."

Heart's desire, heart's desire, heart's desire.

Their words echoed like shouts in a cave, pummeling my ears, piercing my heart.

Granny. I wanted Granny to live.

No, focus, Red! I wanted Goldie. I grabbed a handful of her curls, and her captor reared and hissed, baring mossy teeth.

"Let go, she's mine!" The sprite thrashed and pulled Goldie deeper, taking me with her. I kicked and punched, and in all my flailing I touched the sprite's hand. She grinned malevolently and clamped her cold, webbed fingers around my wrist.

"Now you belong to us!" Their voices echoed in the water, seeping into me. They burrowed into the very depths of my soul.

We hit the bottom of the riverbed. My red cloak billowed around me like red wings. I wished I could fly away. The cloak brushed against my captor. She screamed and released me. Where the cloak had touched her, black blood seeped from her pale skin, clouding the water.

The sprite gnashed her green teeth. She still had Goldie. I pushed forward and thrashed my cloak at her other arm. She screamed again. The other sprites swirled around us, all hissing and shrieking, but they didn't dare come close. I gripped Goldie's curls in one hand and pushed off the bottom of the river toward the surface.

It was so far away. My lungs burned and sparks of white appeared in the corners of my eyes. I'd never make it. Goldie's weight was too much, and my cloak dragged behind me, further weighing me down. Of course. The very thing that had saved us would now bring about our demise.

Something swam toward me. I thought it was another sprite, but it was too dark—all except for the teeth, long white fangs in jaws stretched wide to catch me.

Wolf.

I reached for him, and he grabbed me by the cloak, pulling Goldie and me to the surface.

I gasped for air and held tight to Wolf until I felt earth beneath my feet. I dragged Goldie out of the water and collapsed next to her in the muddy grass. I took deep, ragged breaths, coughing up water, but Goldie didn't move. Her eyes were closed, her lips were blue, and her curls were limp and lifeless, plastered to her pale face.

"Goldie?" I shook her a little, but she still didn't move. "Goldie!" I shook her harder. I smacked her face. Still nothing.

Wolf nudged Goldie's shoulder and whined. *Drowning*, he said.

"But she's out of the water!" I said.

Wolf pushed his paw at her back. *Drowning. Inside. Drowning.* And Wolf showed me an image of water filling up a skin, dry on the outside, but wet on the inside.

I understood. Yes. Goldie's lungs were filled with water. I rolled her onto her side and walloped her on the back. Nothing happened.

More, said Wolf.

So I hit her again. Harder this time, then harder

again, until Goldie coughed and vomited muddy river water. I brushed back her wet curls as she gasped for air. She started to cry.

I let out the breath I'd been holding. "It's okay, Goldie. You're safe now."

Goldie cried and coughed and breathed. When she sat up, I noticed a cut on her arm. She must have scraped it against a rock. I pressed my cloak over it to stop the bleeding while Goldie continued to cry until she caught her breath a little.

"I thought they'd fix things between Mummy and me," she said. "They promised they could make her love me again."

"That's what sprites do," I said. "They lie to make you believe they can grant your heart's desire, and then they drag you down and feed on your wishes."

"But they were so beautiful," she said. "And their voices made me feel safe and warm."

"Yes," I said. "I guess that means beautiful and good are not the same." I removed my cloak from Goldie's arm and inspected her cut. It wasn't too deep. It would heal quickly.

"Then how am I supposed to know who's good?" Goldie asked. "How can I trust anyone?"

How was I to answer such a question? It's true, you can't tell just by looking at someone. You can't always tell by talking to them. And sometimes even the things they do don't speak to their character, because you don't know *why* they're doing them.

"You can't really ever know," I said. "I guess you have to take risks."

"You saved me from the sprites," said Goldie. "You could have died saving me, even when I was so mean to you before."

"I was even meaner to you before that," I said. "You just don't remember."

"What did you do?" she said.

"I made you go away," I said. "I wouldn't let you come with me, even though you just wanted to help."

"Well, that's rude!" said Goldie. She sounded a little more like herself.

"It was," I said, "but that didn't stop you from saving my life the very next day." I lifted the sleeve off my arm and showed her the cut from the bear. "A bear nearly killed me when I tried to get some honey from a honey hive, but you saved me. You must have gotten fifty bee stings to save me."

"Is that why you saved me from the sprite, because I saved you first?"

"I saved you for the same reason you saved me. Because we're friends. Even though you don't remember."

Goldie placed her scratched arm next to mine. Two wounds from two friends saving each other.

"I should like to remember," she said.

"Me too," I said.

Goldie smiled shyly and then yelped as she noticed Wolf. He stood just a few feet away. I could feel his slight fear of Goldie. It made sense, I supposed. When people are afraid of you, it makes you afraid of them, and it's the fear that makes you both dangerous. I suddenly heard Granny's voice in my head.

Don't be afraid, Red.

"Don't be afraid," I said. "Wolf saved us both. We might have drowned without his help."

"Oh," said Goldie, letting out her breath. "Well, then I suppose I ought to thank him, too." She cleared her throat. "Thank you . . . um . . . Mr. Wolf."

Wolf dipped his head in acknowledgment, and then he limped toward me, keeping one of his paws entirely off the ground.

"You're hurt!" I ran to Wolf and inspected him. I couldn't see a wound, but when I touched his leg, he growled a little, then whimpered. I winced as I felt a wave of pain rush through me. "I don't think it's broken," I said. "Maybe just sprained."

He wouldn't be much good for traveling today, and Goldie and I were soaking wet. Now that all the excitement had worn off, we started to shiver.

I looked around for the fire we had built and the rabbit that was surely roasted by now, only to realize that they were on the other side of the river. I could see the smoke from the fire, rising above the trees. We'd have to gather breakfast all over again, though Wolf wouldn't be going on any hunts.

"Let's build a fire," I said. "We can hang our clothes from branches to dry."

I built another fire near the place Wolf was resting. We

took off our sopping clothes, down to our underthings, and hung them on a tree.

"I'm hungry," said Goldie. "I wish we'd caught some fish while we were in the river."

"We still can," I said.

"What about the sprites?" Goldie said. "You can't go in the water!"

"I won't. I have an idea."

Granny had a spell to make the fish jump right out of the water. I'd never tried it before. I always worried I would give myself fins or get swallowed by a fish, but I was feeling bold for the moment. I ran with wolves. I'd just escaped sprites! I could certainly catch a little fish.

I walked to the bank, not too close, but just enough to see a few fish dart by.

Fishing Spell
Come, little fish
Jump on my dish
Swim to shore
Jump and soar
Come, let us meet
And then I will eat

A fish suddenly shot up out of the water. "I got one!" I started to shout, but I only got out "I got!" before the fish plunged right into my mouth, all too eager to become my breakfast. I yanked out the fish and spat and sputtered.

Goldie keeled over laughing, until another fish shot

out of the water and landed on her head, slapping and spraying her with wet fins. "Oh! Ew! Gross! Get it off me!"

"Catch it, Goldie!" I shouted.

The fish fell to the ground, and Goldie pounced on it like a kitten. "I got it! Ooh, gross, these things are slimy!" The fish flopped and slipped from her hands. Meanwhile, two more fish had soared from the river and rained down on the bank. At the end of it all, we had six fish. A feast! Provided by magic that didn't cause anything to break or catch fire.

We huddled by the fire and told stories as we gobbled up the fish. Goldie told a story about three pigs and a wolf that blew down all their houses, except for the one made of bricks. Wolf found this story quite amusing. He thought the wolf was the hero of the tale.

Pigs are delicious, he said.

"I know," I said. "You've been eating Granny's, just like the wolf in the story."

No, said Wolf.

"It's all right, I don't blame you," I said. "We eat them, too."

No pigs, said Wolf, and I realized he was trying to tell me that he had not eaten Granny's pigs.

"But they're gone," I said, "and you're always near Granny's house."

No pigs, Wolf insisted, and he tried to send me an image of something to help explain, but it was hazy and difficult to make out. It didn't matter. They were only pigs. We would have turned them into bacon and ham eventually, so it seemed unfair to begrudge a wild beast his own bacon and ham. As long as the beasts didn't come to eat us, there was no reason to worry.

Wolf, exhausted from his rescue and injury, curled up and fell asleep. I went to see if our clothes were dry, and a movement across the river caught my eye. I shielded my eyes from the sun, and the blood drained from my face. Horst the huntsman was walking slowly through the trees, carefully tracking Wolf's paw prints, with his bow at the ready. He tracked the prints right up to the edge of the bank and then gazed across the river.

I ducked quickly out of sight. I tried not to panic. I didn't think Horst had seen me. He was farther upstream, and anyway, he was on the other side of the river. He had no way of coming over here unless he wanted to swim, which he wouldn't do if he knew anything about sprites.

But none of that stopped Horst. He stood behind a tall tree near the bank and, with one great heave, pushed it over. The tree groaned and fell straight across the river with a crash, creating a bridge over the water.

My jaw dropped. I never would have guessed Horst had the strength for such a thing. Clearly I had underestimated him. Was Wolf in more danger than I'd thought? He most certainly was at the moment.

Horst stepped onto the fallen log and slowly, yet determinedly, started walking across the river.

CHAPTER SIXTEEN

Granny Wolf

Wolf woke as I ran to him. He could sense my terror. His ears went straight up, and the hair at his neck bristled.

"It's Horst!" I whispered.

"Horst? Who's Horst?" said Goldie.

"The huntsman," I said. "He's following Wolf's tracks."

Wolf growled. *Monster!* He tried to get up to run away.

"No!" I said, pushing him down. "He's too close. He'll see you for certain if you try to run, and you can't outrun him with your injured leg." I looked around frantically, searching for a hiding place. Horst was halfway across the river.

I started to gather some leaves and branches to pile over Wolf, but then I caught sight of our clothes drying on the branches, and I got a crazy idea. I snatched some clothes from the tree and quickly went to work. I tied my apron around Wolf's middle and threw Goldie's brown shawl over his shoulders, but that wasn't enough. His ears . . .

"I need to borrow this." I yanked Goldie's frilly cap off her head and stretched it over Wolf's ears. He growled in annoyance.

"I'm sorry," I said, "but it's better than becoming Horst's new wolfskin coat."

Wolf only growled more, cursing. I didn't blame him, of course. Any wolf would naturally dislike a huntsman, and it was possible that Horst had something to do with Wolf's diminished pack. Could he possibly be the monster Wolf spoke of? Wolf's rage rushed through me, and I felt the instinct to attack Horst, but I pushed it down. I couldn't blame Horst, either, could I? It was the way he lived.

"Good day!" shouted Horst. I tried to sit in front of Wolf, blocking him from view as best I could.

"Hello," I said innocently. "Lovely afternoon, isn't it?"

"Yes," said Horst, "though I must say, I'm surprised to see you so far away from the village."

"We just wanted some fresh air," I said, and noticed that Horst looked like he could use some air himself. He had a gray, dusty pallor, and the lines in his face were more pronounced than ever. It was difficult to believe he had just pushed over a tree as easily as I might've snapped a twig in two. Maybe it had been a dead tree, the roots already decayed. Horst took a few stiff steps toward us, his joints cracking with every move.

"And you went for a swim, I see. A little late in the season for that, don't you think, not to mention the perils lurking in the water. Sprites are very dangerous."

"Yes, we saw some sprites," I said. "That's why we got out of the water."

Wolf growled at Horst. I could sense he wanted nothing more than to leap forth and sink his fangs into him, but I held him back.

Horst squinted. "Did I just hear a growl?"

"Oh, that's just Granny," I said. "She's still a little hoarse from her cold, is all."

Horst scratched at his beard. "The witch?" he said. "I came from your granny's just a few hours ago. I was hoping she could help me with something."

My heart leapt. "Is she all right—" I stopped myself. "I mean, yes, Granny has been very ill, but she's getting better, and we decided it would be good for her to get some fresh air."

"Air fresher out here?" Horst asked. "You're a good five miles from home."

"Granny wanted to stretch her legs. She was feeling *very* cramped."

Horst stepped toward Wolf. I held my breath.

"Your granny is looking rather . . . furry."

"That's the medicine I made for her," I told him. "A furry face is one of the side effects."

Horst tugged at the pouch around his neck. "There's a wolf roaming these parts. His paw prints are all around here, and they're fresh."

My heart sped up. "Really? How frightful. We'll have to be very careful, won't we, Goldie?" I nudged Goldie.

"What? Oh, yes, of course. You needn't worry, Mr.

Huntsman. Red is very friendly with wolves. She can even talk— Ouch!"

I pinched Goldie hard.

"What's that you say?" said Horst.

"Nothing. Goldie likes to babble, is all. She's always saying silly things."

"I thought she said something about talking to wolves," said Horst.

I let out a shrill giggle. "Oh, dear, who would talk to a wolf? What would they talk about? Whatever they said would surely be their last words."

Now I was the one babbling. Horst looked at me like I was nuts. "There are some folks known for talking to animals," he said. "Can even befriend them, tell them what to do."

"I hope you find the wolf soon, and we'll be certain to let you know if we see him. Goldie's scream can be heard for miles."

"It can," said Goldie, and she started to demonstrate, but I put my hand over her mouth.

"Don't worry," said Horst. "I've set many traps in the area. He can't escape me forever."

Wolf growled. I dug my hands into his fur to shush him.

"What was that?" said Horst. "Did your granny say something?"

"She said we'll keep our eyes and ears and noses open. Don't worry about us!"

Horst started to leave, then hesitated. "I'm not certain I feel comfortable leaving you ladies all alone here."

Wolf was growling and baring his teeth now. I was having difficulty keeping him down.

"I think I see the wolf!" I shouted, and pointed behind Horst. He jumped around, whipping a knife out of his belt. As luck would have it, a dark tail was indeed sticking out from a shrub. Horst snatched it up.

"Gotcha!" he shouted.

But it wasn't a wolf. It was a skunk! It sprayed right in Horst's face.

Goldie and I covered our noses as the foul odor flooded the air.

But Horst didn't let go of the skunk. He stood stock-still as the skunk finished its business, and then he stomped away into the trees, still clutching the rodent in his fist.

"He must be really hungry," said Goldie.

"At least he won't be able to sneak up on us now," I said. "We'll be able to smell him for miles."

"I think we should go," said Goldie. "I can't stay here another minute with that smell."

"Yes, it would be safer if we left, especially with Horst nearby, though we'll have to go slowly with Wolf's hurt foot."

Wolf jumped up on three legs, growling and tearing at the clothing I had put on him.

"I'm sorry I hurt your wolfish pride," I said, "but at least you're safe."

Monster, said Wolf.

"He's not a monster," I said, "only a huntsman doing what huntsmen do. But I won't let him hurt you, I promise."

Wolf growled a little more. I didn't suppose a wolf and a huntsman could ever be friends.

We started to walk at a slow pace. Wolf kept most of his weight on three legs, but I hoped he'd recover quickly. Who knew when Horst might appear again?

"Where will we go now?" Goldie asked.

"Home, I guess."

"But what about saving your granny? Are you going to give up?"

"No!" I snapped, louder than I'd intended to. Goldie shrank back. I sighed. I had been away from Granny for too long already, but I didn't want to go home empty-handed. I hadn't even managed to get the tree-nymph wings.

Wolf nosed my palm, a gesture of comfort. I rested my hands in his fur, drawing as much comfort as I could.

"I don't know what to do," I finally admitted. "There are the other things the dwarf mentioned—The Red Roses and The Magic Hearts—but I've no idea where to find them."

Goldie slipped her hand into mine. "Then we'll just keep going. You don't always have to know where to look to find what you need."

I wasn't sure what that meant, but I appreciated the sentiment anyway.

❧

We traveled upstream, keeping a watchful eye for traps. I found one snare skillfully hidden just beneath a berry bush, with the kind of berries a wolf might eat when there's no meat around. Humans, too. We gathered the berries and left the trap, but eventually we came upon a trap that was not empty. A creature hung from a branch by its leg, struggling to get free. As we came closer, I heard it talking, cursing in a grouchy, grumbling voice.

"Stupid humans! Filthy mongrels! Spawn of dirt!"

"It's a dwarf!" I cried. And not just any dwarf. *The* dwarf. The very one who had given me directions to the well. I was certain of it. This was luck indeed!

"Oh, no, not *you*!" said the dwarf when he noticed us. "You set this trap, didn't you? You little witch of an ugly girl!"

Wolf growled and snapped his jaws at the dwarf.

"And you brought your beast, eh? Your shadow demon."

"Is that any way to talk to your would-be rescuers? We could get you down, you know, or we can leave you for the huntsman."

"I don't need *you*. I'll get down myself." He felt for his little ax at his side, but it wasn't there. It had fallen to the ground, its blade wedged in a patch of grass.

I picked it up and waved it for him to see. "Looking for this?" He tried to snatch it, but I kept it just beyond his reach.

"I can give you this ax," I said, "if you show me where The Red Roses are."

"Ha! I still don't need you, ugly witch! I can chew my way through these ropes if need be." He tried to bite the ropes, but his feet got tangled in the trap and he fell back, causing the trap to swing wildly.

"Don't worry, Dwarf. The huntsman will set you free

eventually. But his eyes have quite gone, so he might mistake you for a pig and eat you." I sighed dramatically. "Oh, well. Come on, Goldie, Wolf. This dwarf doesn't need us."

We were beginning to walk away when the dwarf called after us. "Oh, all right! All right, ugly human! Get me down and I'll show you to the roses."

"Promise?"

"Yes, yes, now give me my ax."

I handed it to him, and with one swift movement he cut himself free and fell to the ground. Then, quicker than I expected, he started to run away, but Wolf must have seen it coming, because he pounced on the dwarf and pinned him to the ground.

Caught, said Wolf. He looked up at me and wagged his tail, very pleased with himself.

"Thank you, Wolf."

The dwarf wriggled helplessly beneath Wolf's weight, muttering curses and insults. "Evil beast, I'll get you for this! I'll have your teeth and tail!"

I reached for the dwarf, and took him by his pointy black beard. He flailed and twisted and kicked, but I held fast.

"It wouldn't have come to this if you had kept your promise."

"Dwarves don't make promises to humans. You're dirt, filth, putrid giant fleas!"

"I want to get to The Red Roses in the enchanted castle. I request that you take me there yourself." I dropped him, and he immediately ran away, but he didn't go far.

He was bound to keep his promise. What a nasty little brute!

Goldie, Wolf, and I followed as the dwarf led us away from the river, down into a little valley, and then up a grassy hill studded with boulders. He slipped behind a boulder and disappeared. Wolf went after him and a moment later stuck his head out, his tongue lolling like an excited pup's. He must have sensed adventure.

We had to climb a few rocks before we reached the crevice where Wolf and the dwarf stood. "Your friend can't come," the dwarf said, glaring at Goldie.

"What about Wolf?" I asked.

"I can't stop him from coming in, since he's your shadow demon, but I'm only bound to take one ugly girl!"

"We can fix that," I said, snatching the dwarf by the beard once again. I shoved the beard into Goldie's hand. "Goldie, tell him you want him to take you to the enchanted castle."

"Oh, I don't think—"

"Tell him, Goldie, or you'll be left all alone!"

Goldie squeaked, "I want you to take me to the enchanted castle!" and then she dropped the dwarf. "Oh, I'm sorry! Are you hurt?"

The dwarf had gone from radish red to beet purple. He spat at Goldie's feet. "Empty-headed, ghoulish girl!"

"Well, that's not very nice, is it? Further, I don't think it's even truthful. Mummy always said I was witty and pretty as posies."

"And I'm a handsome prince," mumbled the dwarf as

he stepped down into the crevice. It looked dark and deep and rather sinister.

"I don't think we should go down there," said Goldie.

I silently agreed. "Isn't there a way to go aboveground?" I asked.

"I'm sure there is," said the dwarf, "but if you want a guide, then this is the only way. Take it or leave it, and I'd suggest you leave it. There are all manner of deadly dangers down here. Bottomless pits, rivers of fire . . ."

Goldie squeaked, "Oh, please, Red! I don't want to go in there!"

I studied the dwarf. He smiled maliciously. He was probably just trying to throw us off so he wouldn't have to guide us. But he was bound to do it, and I was not that easily frightened. Nor was Wolf.

"Of course we'll go into the tunnel," I said. "I'm not afraid."

The dwarf's smile melted to a sneer. He grumbled insults as he slipped down into the crevice and disappeared. Wolf followed after him.

"Come on." I took Goldie's trembling hand and together we entered the dark cavern.

CHAPTER SEVENTEEN

Dwarf Caverns

The tunnel smelled of stale earth and mold. Within five steps, we were submerged in pitch black. The only thing to guide us was the dwarf's insults echoing from the stone walls. It sounded like there were several dwarves speaking instead of one. I heard the words "ugly," "stupid," "vile," "putrid," "half-wit," and "witch" over and over.

Goldie held tight to my hand, and Wolf walked closely on my other side. His calm gave me reassurance, though the darkness was unsettling. Each step felt treacherous.

"This place is creepy," said Goldie. "Do you think he's trying to get us lost? Or killed?"

"No, he can't." I feigned confidence. "He's bound to take us where we tell— Agh!" I tripped on a loose stone. I caught myself on Wolf, but yanked Goldie down with me, so we tumbled into a heap.

Goldie let loose an earsplitting scream, made ten times louder by the cave. "Help! The cave's collapsing! We're dying!"

"Quiet, Goldie! I only tripped."

Goldie stopped screaming, but she continued to whimper and breathe in short, erratic gasps. "I want to get out of here. I don't like this dark."

"Calm down. As long as we follow the dwarf, we'll be fine."

As soon as I said this, I realized I could no longer hear the dwarf. He had stopped talking. I listened for footsteps but didn't hear any of those, either.

"Dwarf?" I called. "Are you there?"

Goldie clutched my arm. "He left us here to rot!"

"He can't leave us here to rot," I said, but my heart sped up. "Maybe he made a turn and we missed it?"

Follow me, said Wolf, and he pressed on without me.

"Wolf, wait!"

Come, said Wolf. *Don't be afraid.* Then his presence faded from me and I instantly felt exposed and alone. The darkness was so complete I almost felt like I didn't exist, except that Goldie's hand was crushing mine.

"Ouch! Goldie, not so tight!"

"I don't want to die!"

"We're not going to die. We just need to find the wall, and then we should be able to feel our way along the sides of the cave. You take the right side. I'll take the left."

Goldie reluctantly let go of me, and we walked our way along the cave's opposite walls, feeling for any curve or corner that would lead to another tunnel where the dwarf and Wolf might have gone, but we felt nothing.

"I think we should go back. I do not think this is a good ide—*aaaaagh!*" Goldie's scream quickly faded in a way that didn't seem natural, as if she had been swallowed.

"Goldie?" My heartbeat thumped so loudly now it was echoing off the walls. I took another tentative step. Suddenly there was nothing beneath my feet. Cold, dank air whooshed in my ears. I was plummeting down into a deep, dark hole.

Down, down, down, I went, my thoughts and memories rushing up as I descended. And then, in the darkness, I saw the faintest glow and—

Flump!

I landed in a pile of something like sawdust. Lantern light spilled over my surroundings, and I found I had to shield my eyes. Not too far away from me was Goldie, coughing and covered in the black filth of whatever we had landed in. It looked like ashes and soot.

Wolf was at the bottom of the pile, wagging his tail. He was getting around surprisingly well with his injury, only limping slightly. It must not have been as serious as it had seemed back by the river.

The dwarf stood in an entryway, holding a lantern. "Took you long enough," he groused.

"Why didn't you warn us about the fall?" I said, still trying to calm my pounding heart.

"You didn't ask," said the dwarf with a wicked smile.

"It was very rude not to warn us," said Goldie.

"Don't tell me about rudeness," he hissed. "You invoked a curse most abominable to dwarves."

I felt a little stab of guilt for invoking a charm that the dwarf thought of as a curse. Of course it was a curse to him. We forced him to help us when he didn't want to. I should have known better. I'd seen people bound by magic before, and it's no happy thing.

"It's always little girls that take our beards and make us do their bidding," the dwarf continued. "Nasty little witches."

"But what about Snow White?" said Goldie. "The Seven Dwarves were happy to help her!"

The dwarf muttered something like "spoiled brat," and I was suddenly curious how the famous tale of Snow White might be told from a dwarf's point of view. Granny said there were always at least two sides to any story, if not a dozen, and clearly the heroine in the tale was not as beloved by dwarves as we thought. Not by this dwarf anyway. "Let's get moving. I haven't got all day," said the dwarf.

"Wait," I said.

The dwarf turned to glare at me. "Yes, master?"

I winced at his words. I couldn't undo what I'd done, but maybe I could try to make things better.

"What's your name?" The question spilled out of me without thought, but I immediately felt it was the right thing to say. I wasn't sure how meaningful a name was to dwarves, but I had the feeling that calling him "Dwarf" wasn't an endearment.

The dwarf raised his eyebrows. "My name is Borlen."

"I wouldn't have guessed that," said Goldie. "I thought for certain your name was Grumpy."

"That's not a name, you nitwit! It's a putrid human dwarf-insult!"

"Well, if the name fits the destiny . . ." said Goldie.

"Then you'd be called Dopey!" said Borlen.

"That's not—"

"Thank you, Borlen," I said, cutting Goldie off. "We appreciate your help. It means the world to us."

Borlen turned his back on us and walked down the tunnel, still muttering insults, but more softly than before.

The tunnel was narrow and dim, the only light coming from Borlen's lantern. After a series of twists and turns, we entered a huge cavern. "Huge" was not a big enough word, actually, nor was "enormous," "massive," or "giant." It was like a mountain, only inside out.

The air was extremely warm, though I saw no fires except for the torches in sconces on the walls. Ledges and roads zigzagged all along the sides of the cavern, leading to other tunnels. And everywhere there were dwarves. Thousands of them. They bore wheelbarrows and pickaxes, and the cavern echoed with the thumps and pings of mining. It reminded me of the mines on The Mountain, only ten times as big, and the dwarves weren't mining gold, but gems. The wheelbarrows were filled with diamonds, sapphires, emeralds, and crystals of all shades. There were tons of them, heaped up like harvested crops in a field. Some dwarves sorted the gems into bins by their different types and colors. Another team of dwarves poured the gems down chutes, where they were cut and polished and loaded into sacks labeled DEEP-EARTH EMERALDS, CRUSHED CRYSTAL, and FINGERLING SAPPHIRES.

We walked by a pile of gems, and Borlen picked up a pale pink crystal and bit into it like a carrot. He crunched on it, swallowed, and gave a satisfied belch. "I like them raw, right out of the ground," he said, and took another bite.

Goldie and I stared at Borlen. "You *eat* the gems?" said Goldie.

"Of course," said Borlen. "Why else would we spend all our time digging them out of the rock? To *wear* them, like silly humans?"

"But . . . but . . . they're *gems*," said Goldie. "They're very valuable. You could trade them for anything you want!"

"Why would we trade gems when gems are what we want? The only thing I'd trade for is rubies. Rubies are my favorite." His eyes grew hungry.

My hand instinctively flew to Granny's ruby, making sure it was still hidden beneath my dress. I remembered what Granny said about how dwarves love rubies, but I'd had no idea they liked to *eat* them. How awful would it be if Borlen snatched the ruby ring from me and ate it right before my eyes?

"Are there no rubies found here?" I asked, curious.

"They are very rare and valuable to dwarves," said Borlen. "We used to find a small crop of them at least once a month, but their numbers have dwindled over time. It's been years since I've seen a ruby. What I wouldn't give for just one. They have the richest flavor." Borlen closed his eyes, probably imagining a glittering ruby the way I might salivate over a juicy strawberry. Granny's ring felt a little heavier around my neck.

"Come on," said Borlen, returning to his usual grouchiness, as though he'd been neglecting a task. "I could be searching for rubies right now instead of carrying on with you three."

We walked up a narrow ledge. Some of the dwarves stopped and stared, while others glared, clearly understanding the cruel thing we must have done to make Borlen lead us through their caverns. Borlen hung his head in shame as we passed. I felt another stab of guilt.

Further and further we went along the ledge. It turned out there really *were* rivers of fire below us! From high up, we could see them snaking between pillars and bridges of stone, glowing orange and bubbling. No wonder it felt like an oven in here. I guess the dwarves didn't mind the heat, but how could they *live* in a place like this?

"Where do you sleep?" Goldie asked.

"We have homes within the caves," said Borlen.

"With beds and baths and tables and things?"

"Of course. What do you take us for? *Gnomes?*" Borlen grumbled.

We wound in and out of tunnels for what felt like hours. Some tunnels were rough and dull, while others were smooth and shiny, polished by the rivulets of water that snaked down the walls. Some sparkled like millions of tiny gems stuck together, though Borlen told us that was simply an effect of the minerals in the stone. On many caverns, the ceilings and floors had huge stalactites and stalagmites. Sometimes they joined together, creating pillars that made the caves feel like a palace.

"I never imagined the world would look like this underground," said Goldie. "I always thought it would be just dirt and worms."

"It is beautiful," I said.

Borlen suppressed a smile, clearly pleased by our appreciation of his home. "We dwarves have been in these caves for thousands of years, before humans existed."

"Goodness, I never thought there was a time *before* humans," said Goldie.

Borlen scoffed. "Yes, your species thinks quite highly of itself. Think you're kings of the world, don't you? But many noble creatures existed long before you. Your wolf friend comes from a line as ancient as dwarves', and I daresay we'll both still exist long after you run yourselves into extinction. We have gathered more knowledge about the mysteries of the earth than even the most learned humans, even more than witches."

True, said Wolf.

"Well, you don't have to be smug about it," I said to Wolf.

Finally we began to ascend, at last going up instead of in and through and around.

Goldie stumbled and fell at my side. I helped her up, but she resisted and slumped against the side of the tunnel.

"I can't . . . ," she whined.

"We're almost there. Look! I can see light!"

I helped Goldie to her feet, and she leaned on me as we walked toward the pinpoint of light ahead of us.

CRREEEAAKK!

Borlen cursed under his breath. "Hurry," he hissed. "These tunnels can be precarious close to the surface."

We walked as quickly as we could, and the circle of light got bigger and brighter. Pebbles and dust trickled down on us from the ceiling. And then the walls groaned some more and larger rocks started to fall, rocks as big as my head.

"Back! Go back!" Borlen shouted, and we turned to run the other direction. The rocks continued to rain down on us. Borlen dropped the lantern and everything went dark.

"I can't see— Ouch!" said Goldie.

Wolf yelped, and Borlen gasped and groaned, but even though I could sense the rocks coming down on me, I felt no pain.

My cloak. It was protecting me, just as it had protected me against the bear and the sprites.

"Everybody come to me!" I shouted. Goldie and Wolf immediately came and crawled beneath my cloak, but Borlen did not.

"Borlen!" I shouted. I reached out blindly, flapping my arms around until I slapped his head.

"Don't touch me— Agh!" He gasped as more rocks came down.

"I'm sorry, but this is for your own good." I snatched him by the beard and jerked him to me, then spread my

138

cloak over everyone while the rocks showered down. They bounced and rolled off my hood like giant hailstones, and then they grew smaller and fewer until there was nothing more than trickles of dust.

"Is everyone all right?" I asked.

"I th-think so," squeaked Goldie.

"Wolf?" I asked. I felt his nose touch my hand.

"Borlen?" There was a muffled grunt.

"Oh! Sorry!" said Goldie. She shifted, and Borlen gasped for breath. "Are you all right?" Goldie asked.

"Stupid girl, nearly suffocated me to death. Come on," said Borlen. "This way."

"Which way?" said Goldie. "I can't see a thing."

"Follow my voice. Keep your hands to the wall," said Borlen.

"I think we should all stay close to Red," said Goldie. "Just in case there's another cave-in."

"If you keep quiet and move, there won't be one," snapped Borlen.

"Still, it's safer with Red." Goldie took my hand, and Wolf brushed up against my side, and I was glad it was dark, otherwise they would have seen my eyes getting wet. No one had ever told me they felt safer with me before.

We turned a corner, and there was light! Just a faint glow at first, but it got stronger as we walked. I looked at the state of us. We were all covered in dust. Wolf was no longer black, but ashy gray. Goldie's golden curls were grayish brown, but even though my cloak was no longer red, it didn't have a single tear. It was still whole.

We reached a dwarf-sized door. Borlen knocked, and in a few moments another dwarf opened it. This dwarf had twinkly blue eyes, much merrier than Borlen's, and a snowy white beard that reached to his potbelly.

"Borlen!" said the dwarf. "Where in rubies have you been?"

CHAPTER EIGHTEEN
Too Hot, Too Cold, Juuuuust Right

"There was a cave-in," said Borlen, still breathing hard. "Tunnel two hundred and three."

The white-bearded dwarf clicked his tongue. "Third time this century. I suppose we'll have to dig it out again. And what do we have here? A wolf, I see. And humans! Dear Borlen, what are you thinking? You *hate* humans."

"I don't so much anymore," said Borlen sheepishly.

"Of course you do," said the round dwarf. "They took your beard, didn't they?"

"Twice," I said.

"Ha!" The dwarf seemed greatly amused. "I'm Rubald. It's a pleasure to meet you, so long as you don't take me by *my* beard." He chuckled heartily. "Come in! Come in before the rest of the tunnel comes down."

Borlen stepped through the door, followed by Wolf, Goldie, and then me. The ceiling of the entryway was so low I had to hunch over to get in. Eventually it opened up to a larger room just tall enough for me to stand straight, if I didn't mind the roots that dangled from the ceiling brushing the top of my head. The walls were veined with larger tree roots, so we couldn't be too far underground. The sight made me hungry for sky and open space.

Another dwarf stood in the cavern, stirring something in a kettle over a fire. Stewed sapphires, perhaps? Garnet goulash?

"Rumelda! Look who showed up!" said Rubald.

The dwarf by the fire turned around. She had long hair and a round, leathery face, with dark eyes like Borlen's, only hers were softer and warmer.

Rumelda immediately rushed to Borlen and enveloped him in her arms. "My baby! We were so worried."

Borlen tolerated the hug with as much patience as a wriggly toddler. "I'm fine, Mother. Let me go!"

"Your mother!" exclaimed Goldie.

Borlen's mother looked up at Goldie, and her gaze sharpened. "Borlen, my child, why under earth did you bring humans to our home? You hate humans."

"They took him by the beard!" said Rubald cheerfully.

"Oh, not again," Rumelda chided. "Didn't you learn anything the last time this happened? I've told you every day for over two hundred years, you mustn't go aboveground! Rubald, can't you talk some sense into your son?"

"We can't keep him in the cradle forever, Rumelda, dear," said Rubald. "He has to walk on his own two feet sometime, even if it is aboveground."

"But he's frightfully young for such ventures," said Rumelda. "Children reach their hundreds and think they're all grown up and ready to take on the world!"

"How old are you?" Goldie asked, and although I suspected it wasn't very polite to ask, I was curious, too.

"I'm two hundred and seventy-six," said Borlen indignantly.

"Impossible!" protested Goldie. "No one can live that long."

"Huh," said Rubald. "I'm nine hundred and three, and Rumelda's about to crack a thousand."

"Golly grasshoppers!" said Goldie. "You're older than trees! Red, did you know dwarves could live that long?"

"No, I didn't," I said.

"Rubald, it isn't polite to speak of a dwarf's age in front of the humans," chided Rumelda. "It makes them feel perishable."

"Oh, I beg your pardon," said Rubald, but I wasn't offended. My mind buzzed with their centuries of life. Could dwarves live forever? Was there a secret to their long lives? One they might share?

"You must be starving," said Rumelda.

In the center of the room was a squat stone table and three chairs. On the table were three bowls.

"I'm starving!" Goldie ran to the table, snatched a bowl, and started guzzling, then immediately spat out whatever she'd just eaten. Tiny pebbles shot across the room.

"Oh, no, that's far too gravelly!"

She took the next bowl and tried to take a sip but abruptly put it down.

"Rock solid!"

"Try this one, dear." Rumelda set another bowl on the table. It was full of grayish-brown goop.

Goldie took a sip and smacked her lips, then drained the bowl in five seconds and finished with a belch. "It could use a touch of honey, but it slides down well."

The three dwarves gaped at her.

"Why don't we sit down for supper?" said Rumelda, politely ignoring Goldie's rudeness.

"Oh, yes, my legs are about to fall off." Goldie flopped herself in one of the chairs and squirmed, then moved to another. She tested all the chairs until she settled in a little golden rocker and relaxed. "Oh, yes. Yes, this is perfect." She rocked back and forth.

"But . . . but . . . ," stuttered Borlen.

"There, there, dear," said Rumelda. "I've made your favorite tonight. Roasted sapphires."

"That's not my favorite," said Borlen, and I knew he was wishing for rubies. Granny's ring seemed to prick my chest.

Meanwhile, Rumelda served Borlen and Rubald the sapphires like a pile of roasted vegetables, then dished out three bowls of the goopy stuff Goldie had slurped up before. They called it *strolg.* "Your weak stomachs can't handle our gems, I know," said Rumelda. "But any creature can eat strolg, even wolves."

The strolg was a very salty sort of porridge with a dusty

aftertaste, but at least it went down easily. Goldie downed another bowl in five seconds and asked for more, after which she launched into her usual heap of questions.

"Do dwarves *only* eat gems, or do you have other foods as well, such as wood chips? Coal? And how does that affect your . . . *inner workings?*"

The dwarves' cheeks became noticeably red.

I choked on the strolg. "Goldie, you can't ask *that*."

"Why not? Mummy says if there's something we don't know, we should always ask, otherwise how would we learn anything?"

"I don't think that advice includes questions about anyone's inner workings."

"Of course it does. How many living things do you know that can eat rocks? I find it fa—ah—ascinating," Goldie yawned. "Excuse me, I'm so sleepy all of a sudden."

"You are welcome to rest in one of our beds," said Rubald, "though you may not find them to your liking."

The dwarf beds were actually little alcoves carved right into the walls. Goldie crawled into one and quickly got out. "How can anyone sleep there? I can feel the rocks poking me."

"Works out the kinks in my back," explained Rubald.

Goldie crawled into the next alcove and promptly slid out because the stones were so smooth. "That doesn't seem safe."

"I'm a light sleeper," said Rumelda.

Borlen piped up, "Just stay out of my—"

But Goldie had already crawled into the third bed,

which was the smallest, and she immediately curled up into a ball and wrapped her shawl around her like a blanket. "Oh, yes, this is cozy." She was asleep in moments.

Borlen looked dumbfounded. "There's a human in my bed."

Rubald laughed gleefully.

"There, there, Borly, dear," cooed Rumelda. "I'll make you a cozy bed on the floor next to mine."

With Goldie asleep, it became very quiet, and I realized that all three dwarves had their attention on me.

"So," said Rubald. "What brings you to our caverns? Only a very knowledgeable human would know to take a dwarf by the beard, and only a very strange request would bring you through our caves."

"I asked Borlen to take me to the enchanted castle," I said, "to find The Red Roses."

Rubald nodded. "We dwarves have long admired the castle. The gargoyles have ruby eyes, and it's said to be full of magical wonders, such as The Red Roses that you seek."

"Then you've used them!" I said excitedly. "That's why dwarves live so long, isn't it?" Oh, it would be perfect knowing that one could use the roses without too many ill effects. Maybe the enchantment was what made the dwarves eat rocks. That would be okay, wouldn't it? Eating rocks in order to live longer seemed a fair trade. Or maybe the roses were what made the dwarves *dwarves*. Would Granny mind being a dwarf and eating rocks? Would I?

But Rubald shook his head. "Dwarves have long lives naturally. We've never desired eternal life, so we don't seek it. Our gems keep us strong for a good long time. When we reach the end, we're content to go to sleep and turn to dust and stone, maybe even gems."

I made a face. "So . . . dwarves eat *each other?*"

Rubald laughed. "When humans die, they turn to dirt and all kinds of edible plants that grow out of the dirt. So I suppose you could say we're all eating each other. Life moves in continuous circles."

"It doesn't feel that way," I said. "Not when someone dies."

"Let me show you something." Rubald walked behind me and stood directly in front of a wall. I hadn't noticed before, but the walls of the cave were covered with drawings and writing: maps, drawn with astonishing detail. There were paths twisting around trees, climbing mountains, and reaching to different destinations, most of which I'd never heard of, such as *The Boiling Bogs* and *The Serpentine Seas* and *The Hidden Islands.* Some paths had written directions, such as *Take seven steps to the left after reaching the cliffs* and *Don't eat the yellow berries. Poison.* It reminded me of Granny's table, with all her recipes etched into the wood.

I traced my path to the stream where I had met Borlen, down the river and the mountain to *The Wine Well,* which was also marked, and then back up the river to where we were now, in *Dwarf Caverns* and, more specifically, *HOME,* marked with a circle and a red *X.*

Farther down the wall, I found my home. There was the village, the mine, and even Granny's house—a little cottage labeled *The Witch of The Woods.*

I placed my hand over Granny's house and felt a deep pang of missing her. How much deeper would the hurt be if she were gone forever!

"You humans seem to fear the end of life," said Rubald, as though he were reading my thoughts. "It is a curse to you, no?"

"It's . . . not a pleasant thing," I said. "If there were a way to keep living, I think that would be better."

"And so you seek The Red Roses," said Rubald.

"I seek a way to save Granny," I said. "We tried The Wine Well, but that went all wrong. Goldie drank the wine and lost a bit of her memory, you see."

"Borlen!" shouted Rumelda. "Did you send these girls to The Wine Well on purpose?" Borlen looked away from his mother, face flushed. "You naughty little dwarf! You *knew* what would happen if they drank it!"

"So?" he said. "They took me by the beard!"

"And that's your own fault for going aboveground. No, you apologize this instant." She grabbed him by the beard herself and set him down before me.

Borlen glared at his feet in defiance. "Sorry," he spat.

"If anyone should apologize, it's me," I said. "It was rude of me to take you by the beard. I realize that now. But I still need your help. You mentioned another way, too, besides The Red Roses. You called it The Magic Hearts? But I don't see that anywhere on the map."

Rubald stiffened. Rumelda gasped. "Borlen, you didn't!"

Borlen crossed his arms. "I didn't tell her anything except a name, and besides, there's nothing to tell. We don't know any more than that, not really."

"I don't understand," I said. "Do the hearts exist?"

"Oh, yes," said Rubald. "But . . ." Rubald glanced at the maps. "I'm not certain The Witch of The Woods would prefer that particular magic. What do you think, Borlen? You met her."

Borlen's eyes narrowed at Rubald.

"What do you mean? You don't mean Granny . . ."

"Didn't she ever tell you about a dwarf she once met and took by the beard?"

I nodded. "You mean it was . . ."

"It was Borlen!" said Rumelda. "Must have been seventy years ago, when Borlen was just out of the cradle—little troublemaker snuck away from me the first chance he got, and then got caught by a witch!"

"She stole my gems!" said Borlen.

"That's not right," I said. "Granny said the dwarf stole gems from a prince! Granny was just taking them back."

"The prince stole the gems from *me*," snapped Borlen. "So I was taking them back from the prince, and then your *dear* granny took me by the beard and made me give them to her!"

"Why would a prince steal gems? He's a *prince*."

Borlen raised one eyebrow. "Have you never heard of a greedy royal?"

I swallowed my words. I certainly had. King Bartholomew Archibald Reginald Fife was as greedy as they come. His greed had nearly destroyed The Kingdom. It completely destroyed him, but that is a different tale.

"Your granny wouldn't even listen to my side of the story," said Borlen.

My head whirled. Granny hadn't told me any of this. I was starting to wonder what other things I didn't know about Granny.

"I'm sorry my granny caused such trouble for you. I'm sorry *I* caused so much trouble."

Borlen gave a grunt that sounded like an acceptance of my apology.

"Now, what of The Magic Hearts? Can you tell me anything?"

Rubald and Rumelda shared a look. "We've only heard rumors, so we know nothing for certain. Only those who have actually used the magic would know."

"It's Borlen's bedtime," said Rumelda, clearly ready to end the conversation. "You've had far too much excitement for one day." Borlen grumbled and yawned at the same time.

Wolf was curled up near the fire, and Goldie was snoring in Borlen's bed. Rumelda placed a slab of rock at the side of her bed for Borlen, then tucked him in among flat stones as though they were fluffy pillows. She sang him a lullaby about a girl who cut through ten miles of stone to find a single ruby and then lived ten thousand years. Borlen fell asleep with a peaceful smile on his face.

Rubald and I sat in silence for a while as Rumelda went about readying herself for bed. Eventually he spoke in a thoughtful voice.

"Death can be a hard thing, even for dwarves," said Rubald. "When a young dwarf dies, even at a hundred years, we mourn greatly." He looked at Borlen as he spoke, and sighed. "I suppose I can empathize with your quest, though we dwarves have a saying: 'Let the rocks fall where they may.' It means sometimes we must allow things to happen as they will."

"And sometimes we have to fix things," I said. "Sometimes we have to stop bad things from happening."

"We are both right," said Rubald. "The true wisdom lies in knowing what we can fix and when we must let go."

I didn't have the energy to respond. All I knew was that I couldn't give up. Granny wasn't a rock that I could toss aside. She was a precious gem to me, like a ruby to a dwarf, one that I needed very badly.

I lay down next to Wolf and curled my head in the crook of his stomach. He placed a paw on my shoulder.

"Good night, Wolf," I whispered.

Wolf's ears twitched a little, and I felt his contentment. It washed through me, loosened all the knots inside my head, and I fell into a soft, restful slumber.

CHAPTER NINETEEN
Roses Are Red, Gargoyles Are True

Hours later, I was kicked awake by Borlen. "It's time to go," he growled.

I yawned and stretched and so did Wolf. Goldie was still asleep and snoring in Borlen's bed, something that seemed to be causing him no small amount of distress. He poked and prodded her and even yanked her curls, then finally tugged at her shawl until she tumbled to the floor.

Goldie's eyes fluttered open. She sat up and stretched. "I've never slept so well in all my life," she declared.

Borlen grumbled and crunched on a few emeralds. Rumelda had prepared more strolg for the rest of us. I drank it down quickly and thanked her and Rubald for their kindness.

"You are welcome here," said Rumelda. "Even if you

don't take Borlen by the beard—though it serves him right, always going to the surface."

Borlen took us back through the cave tunnels with a fresh lantern, and in less than an hour we had emerged aboveground. The sun was just rising, and after spending so many hours in the dim caves, I had to shield my eyes against the brightness.

"We're not far from the castle," said Borlen. "It's just down this stream and past those hills."

As we walked along the stream, Goldie and I washed the dust and grime off ourselves as best we could. Wolf rolled around in the water until he was black again, then shook his fur so it splattered all over Borlen.

"Filthy mongrel!" grunted Borlen, though I secretly suspected he'd grown fond of Wolf.

We came to a steep hill. The stream disappeared into a tunnel, and we walked up the hill. We reached the top and saw that a valley lay below. The stream trickled out into a shining lake, and on the other side of the lake was a castle. The morning mist hung thick in the little valley below, with the castle towers and turrets peeping through like they were rising out of a cloud.

"There is your enchanted castle," said Borlen.

"Oh, how glorious!" said Goldie. "Wouldn't you like to live there, Red? We could be queens!"

"Thank you, Borlen," I said. "You've been very kind." Borlen raised an eyebrow and turned to leave.

"Wait," I said.

"Another demand?" he asked coolly.

I pulled out my ring and yanked it from the chain about my neck. I instantly felt a weight being lifted.

"Here." I placed the ruby ring in Borlen's hand. "This is for you."

He stared at it. His beard twitched. "But . . . this is very valuable to you."

"It's a silly thing . . . humans wearing rocks when there are those who could eat them."

"Yes, very foolish." Borlen gave me a smile, one that was warm and kind instead of sharp and sinister. He tucked the ring inside his pocket, not his pouch. I had a feeling he wouldn't eat it.

"Good luck with your enchanted castle and roses," said Borlen.

"Take care of your beard," I said.

Borlen bowed respectfully to us, and then he went back down the hill while Goldie, Wolf, and I went down the opposite side, toward the enchanted castle.

The mist surrounding the castle was so thick I could barely see Wolf walking in front of me, but I could smell the roses. The air was drenched with their perfume. You could taste it when you breathed.

The castle was surrounded by a stone wall with heavy iron gates overgrown with thorny vines. They opened as we approached.

"That's friendly," said Goldie.

"Creepy, more like," I said.

Wolf growled. He felt threatened.

We walked through the gates and entered a garden smothered in roses. Drowning in roses. Creamy white, butter yellow, perfect pink, and dusky lavender. They grew around statues and stone benches, cascaded over bridges and trellises, and climbed the castle walls.

Goldie sniffed each blossom she passed. "Such lovely roses! I could take a bouquet of these to Mummy and she'd be overcome with love." Goldie sniffed and sniffed until I was certain she was intoxicated.

I saw no Red Roses, but that wasn't surprising. Magic roses wouldn't be sitting in plain sight, and they'd likely be protected. Granny protected her garden from pests with a repellent spell. She called it a respellent.

Respellent
Crawly critters of The Woods
Keep out of my garden goods
Do not try to nosh and nibble
Lest we have a little quibble

If any creature did try to nosh or nibble, the magic prevented them from eating for at least a full day. A squirrel's teeth would grow too big for its mouth. If a worm or caterpillar managed to creep into an apple, the bug would swell up so big it couldn't get out, and if a beetle landed on a cabbage or tomato, its head would pop into its body like a turtle's.

I pulled the hood of my cloak over my head, hoping I'd never have to find out what it feels like to have your head pop outside in.

I left Goldie to her sniffing and walked toward the center of the garden, closer to the castle. It was a grand and imposing thing, bigger than the castle in The Kingdom, and hewn out of smooth stone. The towers and ledges were adorned with ruby-eyed gargoyles. Wolf growled. *Danger.*

"They're stone," I said, but I gathered my cloak tighter still, trying to shield myself from a sudden chill.

We went through a maze of roses. Pale peach, deep violet, white with pink tips, and yellow with orange tips. There were even blue roses, but no red ones.

After a time, we came to a tall hedge that grew in a circular fashion, the vines and branches so closely knit you couldn't see a single thing beyond them. We walked all around it. There was no opening. I got down on my hands and knees and wiggled between the thorny branches just enough to see a flash of red. My heart leapt.

"They're here," I whispered. "Wolf, help me dig a hole to get through."

Wolf whimpered, backing away. He didn't like thorns.

"Don't be a 'fraidy wolf," I said, but he wouldn't help me. "Fine, I'll do it myself." I steeled my nerves and went to war with the roses. They put up a good fight, scratching my face and hands, snagging my cloak, but I fought back. I tore my way through until I tumbled out the other side of the bushes and landed on all fours. Wolf cleared the hedge with one spectacular leap. He landed next to me with an expression that could only be described as smug.

"Show-off," I muttered.

I stood, brushing the dirt and leaves from my clothes, then stilled as I took in the view before me.

Roses. Red Roses. The reddest I'd ever seen.

At first glance, they looked like ordinary flowers, but as I drew closer, I detected a soft glow around the edges that pulsed like a beating heart. They hummed with life and smelled of transformation.

I reached out to pick one, then paused. Something rustled close by.

Snap!

"Who's there?" I asked.

"Ooh! Ouch! You nasty roses!"

"Goldie?" I called. Her voice sounded near.

"Ooooouuch! Red! The roses have captured my curls and they won't let go!"

I chuckled softly. "Hang on!" I called to her. "I'll be there in a minute."

I turned back to The Red Roses.

I wrapped my hand in my cloak, feeling I was not supposed to touch the rose myself. It could upset the magic, and I wanted it to be perfect for Granny.

I reached for the rose again. There was more rustling, noticeably closer this time.

Wolf started to whimper and paw at the ground.

Danger.

"Hush," I whispered. "It's just a bird or something." But my heart was beating fast now. Time to take what I needed and leave. I took hold of one of the thorny stems and snapped it off the bush. I'd done it! I had a Red Rose!

"Let's go," I said.

Something crashed to the ground before me. Dirt sprayed up in my face. I turned and shielded myself when another boulder-like object came down to my right, falling from the sky. Another crashed down, and another, and another, until Wolf and I were surrounded by . . . gargoyles!

The stone demons were alive. They had curled horns, flared nostrils, and pointed, bony wings. Their ruby eyes glowed as they flapped their wings and gnashed their stone teeth. They crawled on hands and feet, closing in on Wolf and me. Wolf growled and snapped at them, baring his fangs. I clutched the fur at his neck, trying to swallow the fear crawling up my throat.

"It's all right," I said. "They can't hurt us. My cloak will protect us."

One gargoyle pounced on Wolf, and they snarled and wrestled on the ground while the others continued to crawl toward me on all sides. I whipped my cloak at the monsters. It had protected us before. It had stung the water sprites, and shielded us from the falling rocks, but it seemed to have no effect on the gargoyles. They crept closer, stone tongues licking their curled lips.

Wolf was still fighting, biting and clawing at the gargoyle, but it didn't so much as flinch. How could he harm a stone gargoyle? They're not made of flesh and bone and blood.

If Granny were here, she'd perform a charm that would turn the gargoyles back to rigid stone, but I feared I'd turn myself to stone if I tried the same thing.

The gargoyles were inches from me. One tore the Red

Rose from my hand and flung it to the ground. Two more lifted me up by the arms and flew me over the hedge.

"Stop!" said a voice, and the gargoyles halted mid-flight, dropping me to the ground. I turned to see a tall figure in a black hood walking toward me. It seemed to be a man, but his gait was strange, like he was lame or injured. Still, whoever it was clearly had command of the gargoyles. Here was someone who could free us.

But then he removed his hood, and the blood drained from my face. The man was not a man at all. His face was covered in matted fur. His long nose blended with his forehead like a cat's. His lips were black, and fangs curled down over his chin more grotesquely than the gargoyles'.

"What are you doing in my garden?" he said in a deep, growling voice.

"I need a rose. For my granny. She's sick."

"And so you thought you'd steal from me?"

Wolf came bounding across the garden. He attacked the beast, clawing and biting him, but the beast flung him off. The gargoyles pounced on Wolf like feral cats.

"Wolf!" I struggled against the gargoyles, but the beast knocked me to the ground and held me down with one paw. His claws dug into me like daggers.

"Leave him alone!" I shouted.

"No one touches my roses!" the beast roared.

"He didn't touch them! I did! You have so many I didn't think it would matter."

"My roses matter a great deal," said the beast, and I knew he was talking about their magic. He knew the power they had, and he wanted to keep it all to himself.

"Please!" I begged. "My granny is dying!"

"Then go home and say your goodbyes," said the beast. "That's what humans do. Take her away!"

A gargoyle snatched me up once again and started to carry me away. Away from The Red Roses. Now I was certain these roses would save Granny. I was so close.

"But her name is Rose!" I shouted. "Rose Red! The Red Roses are her destiny! Please!"

"Stop!" said the beast, and the gargoyle obeyed. "Put her down." The gargoyle released me instantly, so I fell hard to the ground. "What did you just say?" the beast demanded.

"My granny," I said. "She's sick."

"No. Her name. What was the name you just said?"

I swallowed. This was the crucial moment. It would either tip things in my favor or against me. "Rose," I said. "Sometimes she is called Rose Red, and sometimes she is called The Witch of The Woods."

The beast was still, as were the gargoyles, as though the name had cast some kind of spell. "You are . . . her grandchild, this Rose Red?" said the beast softly.

I nodded. "Her only grandchild. Please, she's very ill. She'll die if I don't bring her a rose, and she can't. She can't die."

The whole world was quiet, holding its breath, until the beast spoke.

"Get rid of the wolf," he commanded.

"No!" I shouted. "Let him go! Don't hurt him!" I tried to stand, but the gargoyles held me in place. I could hear Wolf growling and snarling.

"Wolf, run!" I shouted. "Don't fight! Run!"

Wolf yelped. He was tossed up into the air just high enough that I caught a glimpse of him, and then the gargoyles carried him away while the beast lifted me off the ground with one arm like I was nothing but a kitten. Caught.

"I'm free!" I heard Goldie shout.

Goldie! I had forgotten. I couldn't see her. I hoped the beast couldn't, either. She was my only hope.

"Goldie! Run! Run and get help!"

"It's okay. I don't need help anymore. I beat those beastly roses!"

I saw Goldie's curls bouncing above the rosebushes. She was running right toward the beast!

"Goldie, turn around! Run the other way!" Goldie stopped and turned around, but the gargoyles flew over the rosebushes and blocked her path. She screamed and curled up into a ball. The beast leapt over the hedge with incredible power and speed. He scooped up Goldie and carried us both, one underneath each arm, dangling sideways.

"Oh, Red!" Goldie shrieked. "Have we been caught by a bear?"

She was staring at the beast's feet, which were not feet at all, but giant, hairy paws with razor-sharp claws.

"No, it's not a bear," I said.

The beast bounded up a stone staircase to a set of large double doors that swung open on their own and shut as soon as we had entered.

We were now prisoners of a beast.

CHAPTER TWENTY

The Beast's Feast

The beast locked us in the room and left without a word. Goldie scrambled to the door and pounded. "Please!" she cried. "I'll never see Mummy again! I'll never be loved!" She rattled the door handle, then slid down to the floor and lay in a puddle of tears.

I sat next to Goldie, too shocked to cry. A memory flashed through my head of the last time I'd been imprisoned in a castle, with Rump. It had been his own magical mess that had brought us there. This time I had no one to blame but myself, and it was up to me to get us out.

I took stock of the room. It was not a cell or a cage, but a very decent bedroom with two beds. The bedspreads were embroidered with roses, red on one, yellow on the other, as though the beast had known ahead of time that Goldie and I were coming—or the castle had.

I went to the window and searched the castle grounds

for any sign of Wolf. Did he escape? Could I escape? Not likely. We were very high off the ground, and there were no trees near the window.

A clock ticked on the wall. It was in the shape of a rose, a red one. The red petals splayed evenly outward, with thorny stems and leaves in place of the hands. The clock ticktocked a thousand times. When the longer stem reached the top of the hour, a little door opened and a bird emerged and chirped as though delivering a message, but nothing happened. The beast did not come.

"What do you think the beast will do with us?" Goldie asked.

"I don't know."

"Do you think he means to eat us?" Goldie asked.

"Perhaps," I said. "Though in that case, he probably would have brought us to the kitchen or the cellar."

The clock chirped again and again. We'd been locked in the room for five hours, according to the little bird.

"I'm hungry," said Goldie just as the door clicked and swung open. No one entered.

"Do you suppose there's a ghost in this castle?" Goldie quivered.

"Maybe." I walked to the door and peered out. There was no one there. I took a step out of the room.

"Don't go!" Goldie squeaked. "What if the ghost gets you?"

"Would you rather stay locked up in the room?"

"No," said Goldie.

"Then come on. Remember how the castle gate let us in? Maybe the castle will let us out. Maybe it's on our side." Goldie dried her eyes and got to her feet. As soon as we stepped out of the room, the door shut and locked again, so we could not go back. Somehow it felt more disconcerting to be locked out than in.

To our right, there was a solid stone wall. There was only one way for us to turn, and that was left. We walked down the corridor, and as we did, the sconces on the wall lit up their candles all on their own.

"Definitely ghosts," said Goldie, clinging to me so tightly her nails left little half-moons in my skin.

"Not ghosts," I said. "Magic. It's an enchanted castle, remember?" And I had to admit, it was good magic, or at least skilled magic. Even the gargoyles, though terrifying, were impressive. Only a very powerful witch or magician could have performed such spells and enchantments. Was it the beast who had cast them?

The corridor ended at a large staircase, leading down to the foyer and main doors. There was no sign of the beast. No sentries or servants stood guard. Goldie and I looked at each other, then raced down the stairs, ran to the door, and turned the knob. We pulled and pushed, but it was locked and would not budge.

"I suppose the castle isn't really on our side," said Goldie. It made my chest pinch to see Goldie so forlorn. She was like a butterfly without its wings.

"We'll find another way out," I said, trying to sound cheerful and not at all worried. "And while we're looking, we can explore the castle. Not everyone gets to see inside a castle, especially an enchanted one."

Goldie brightened a little. "True. I've always wanted

to live in a castle, though as a princess, not the prisoner of a beast."

"Picky, picky," I chided.

A door to our right opened up with a creak that almost sounded like an invitation to come inside. We entered an enormous sitting room with lots of cushioned chairs and intricately carved tables. On the tables sat vases filled with withered roses.

"You'd think the beast would at least bring in fresh flowers," said Goldie. "He certainly has enough."

"Red! Red! Red!" a voice squawked. I turned around to find a very colorful bird inside a golden cage. I'd never seen a bird like this. She was green with blue-tipped wings and spoke much like a regular person would speak. "Red! Red! Red!" she squawked over and over.

"She knows your name!" said Goldie.

"Goldie! Goldie! Goldie!"

"Galloping grasshoppers! She knows my name, too! I wonder if she can tell us how to escape. Please, pretty bird, can you tell us how to get out of the castle?"

"Trapped, trapped, trapped!" the bird said. "Red! Goldie! Red! Goldie! Trapped!"

"That's not very helpful," said Goldie.

On the west side of the room was a large stained-glass window with a picture of a beautiful woman. Dark, soft curls framed her face. She wore a blue gown and a silver crown with a sapphire at the center of her forehead. The late-afternoon sun poured through the panes, spilling colored light on the dusty floor of the castle. There was something strange about the woman in the window, as though she were somehow enchanted, too. Her eyes were too life-like, her gown seemed softer than glass should look, and the sapphire sparkled like a real stone rather than colored glass. I wondered who she could be.

I walked around, gazing at the odd little figurines, instruments, and curious boxes, but I was careful not to touch anything. I could feel the magic coursing through the walls. It tingled in my fingers, buzzed in my ears, and made my hair stand on end. There were dozens of enchantments and spells in this room alone, all woven together, and tugging at just one string might unravel a tapestry of chaos.

"Red, look at this!" Goldie pointed at a peacock-feather quill that was writing all on its own. It dipped itself in an inkpot and wrote in elegant calligraphy on cream-colored paper atop a small desk.

Supper is served in the dining hall.
Your master awaits. . . .

Goldie reached out for the quill.

"Goldie, don't touch it!"

Too late. She balled her fist around the quill and began scribbling on the page. "Are you a ghost?" She spoke aloud as she wrote. "Can you help us escape— Ouch!" The pen had wrenched itself free of Goldie's grasp and poked her hand.

Do not keep the master waiting.
The consequences can be quite nasty.

Speaking of nasty, you have a booger hanging from your nose. You will find a handkerchief in the drawer of this desk.

Goldie's hand flew to her nose. "How rude! But do I really have a booger hanging from my nose?" She lifted her chin for me to see.

"Yes."

"Why didn't you say something?" Goldie opened the drawer and found a white handkerchief with a rose stitched onto the corner. She wiped her nose and began to place the handkerchief back inside the drawer when the pen wrote again.

You may keep it. I'm not fond of gifts from the nose. Only from the heart.

"It's a rather impertinent pen," said Goldie.

"But smart," I said, quite fascinated with the writing pen.

Goldie sighed. "Let's find the dining hall. I'm hungry, and something smells good."

Just as she said that, a door swung open to our right, and the smell intensified, strong and inviting. Roasted meat and herbs and onions. Garlic. Butter. Bread. We were led by our noses until we found the source of the delicious smell.

We arrived in an elegant dining hall. The table was loaded with a dozen different dishes, all of them steaming and fragrant. Silver plates had been set out, and flickering candles lit the room.

The beast sat at the head of the table. He had already begun to eat, tearing into a leg of lamb and crunching on the bone while the juices ran down his matted fur. When he noticed Goldie and me, he wiped his mouth with a furry paw.

"Sit," he said, gesturing to the two seats on either side of him.

When we sat, a silver tureen lifted off the table and ladled steaming soup into our bowls. It was a red tomato soup.

"Eat," the beast commanded.

Goldie began to eat hers immediately, but I didn't. I didn't think it was poisoned, but I didn't like the way the beast ordered us about, expecting us to obey like dogs.

"I'm not hungry," I said.

"Yes, she is," said Goldie. "We're starving. We haven't eaten since this morning with the dwarves, and they eat rocks."

I glared at Goldie and clenched my jaw. "I'm not hungry."

The beast glared at me. "Eat," he said, his voice low and dangerous.

I said nothing, only glared back. He didn't look away, and neither did I, so we were caught in a glaring contest. I have never lost a glaring contest, and I thought I was winning until the beast roared so loudly and fiercely that a wind rushed at my face and blew out several of the candles. I'd be lying if I said that didn't frighten me, but I couldn't show it. This was a battle of wills. I took my silverware as though to eat, but as soon as the beast started to relax, I stabbed the knife and fork into the table and folded my arms over my chest.

The beast jumped upon the table, upsetting dishes and goblets and the tureen of tomato soup. He shoved his face inches from mine. "You think you're brave, do you?" he said. "But only those with the deepest fears come for my roses, so perhaps you're not so brave after all?"

I flinched involuntarily. Goldie had frozen, her face splattered with tomato soup and her spoon perched on the tip of her tongue.

The beast clambered down from the table, crushing a pie and demolishing a loaf of bread.

A tense silence filled the room. The beast went back to attacking his food while glaring at me. After a while, Goldie chirped up with her usual chatter.

"This food is delicious," she said. "Did you make it?"

"No."

"Then you must have a wonderful cook," said Goldie.

"No."

"Your mummy?"

"No."

"Your wife, then?"

The beast choked on a bone. "No. My castle provides everything I need."

"Ooh, how wonderful! Could your castle by chance make golden apple tarts? My mummy makes the most wonderful golden apple tarts. I doubt even a magic castle could make them better."

The beast scratched at his furry chin, clearly unsure what to make of Goldie.

"What's your name?" Goldie asked. "You never did tell us."

"Beast," said the beast.

"Of course, but what is your *real* name? The one your parents gave you. Surely they didn't name you Beast."

The beast growled, showing sharp teeth.

"Beast is a perfectly suitable name." Goldie slurped her soup. When her bowl was empty, a knife and fork sliced some mutton and placed it on her plate while a spoon scooped her some potatoes and beets. My stomach growled noticeably, but I still did not touch the food.

Goldie asked a dozen questions about the castle—how it worked, what other things it could do besides cook, and if Beast thought the castle might be able to make her mummy love her. The beast mostly answered "No" or "I don't know" with increasing agitation, until I feared he would explode again, so I changed the subject.

"How long do you intend to keep us, Beast?" I demanded.

"Until I get what I want," he said.

"What do you want?"

"The return of what was stolen from me."

"But I didn't steal anything. Your gargoyles took the rose."

"Yes, the rose," he said. "You wished to bring one to your granny, The Witch of The Woods, you said? And if she is truly a witch, wouldn't she know of such magic herself?"

"Yes," I said. "But she's too ill to perform such powerful magic."

"And you, her granddaughter, cannot perform such magic? Did she not teach you?"

I felt my face heat up. "She hasn't taught me everything."

"Red's very afraid of magic," Goldie said with her mouth full of bread. "She nearly killed her granny!"

Beast's ears twitched. "Nearly killed your granny! How charming." He tore off a final strip of meat and tossed the bone aside. A pitcher poured wine into his goblet, and he guzzled it down.

"What will you do with us?" I asked.

"Make you my servants, of course."

"Your servants?" I said. "What for? You just told us your castle takes care of all your needs."

The beast casually observed one of his claws. "An enchanted castle takes all the fun out of being in charge. I miss giving orders and having them grudgingly obeyed. You two will fill the hole in my heart." He rose from the table, brushed some bread crumbs off his fur, then brushed all the scraps from the table onto the floor.

"Now clean up this mess." With a swirl of his cloak, he strode out of the dining hall. The doors shut behind him.

Goldie and I sat still, trying to make sense of the bizarre moment. "At least he's not going to eat us," said Goldie.

My stomach screamed. With the beast gone, it didn't seem beneath me to eat something. I reached for my spoon, but it slid out of my fingertips. I tried to lift my bowl to drink from it, but it jerked and splashed soup in my face.

"Grrrrrr!" I growled and clawed for any food within my reach, but it all jumped and slid away from me. The knife and fork crossed themselves in front of the mutton.

"I guess supper is over?" said Goldie. "I think we're supposed to clean up."

"That beast can't make me do anything." I huffed to the door and turned the knob, but it didn't open. I marched to the door on the other side of the room, but it wouldn't budge, either. It wasn't until Goldie started stacking dishes on a tray that a door clicked and swung ajar. That door led us to the kitchen, which was piled high with pots and pans waiting to be washed.

I groaned.

"It's not so bad." Goldie pushed up her sleeves. "We can get this done quick as pixies if we work together."

But washing dishes in an enchanted castle was not as easy as Goldie had predicted. When we started to wash them, the dishes wrenched themselves out of our hands and smashed against the walls and ceiling, spraying shards of china all over. We tried again, with the same result.

"I think they're ticklish," said Goldie.

They were definitely something. We had to wash them only in a circular motion with just the right amount of pressure, otherwise they went mad and we had even more of a mess to clean. But the worst was washing the pots and kettles. I accidentally scrubbed too hard on a big black kettle, the kind in which Granny would brew a potion, and it turned itself over on my head, drenching me with dirty dishwater. Goldie burst into giggles. My only consolation was that she slipped up with her own pot and got the same treatment.

After the dishes were washed, we were guided by the castle back to our room. On the beds lay two white nightgowns, one with red roses and one with yellow roses stitched on their hems.

Goldie went behind the screen to change and exclaimed, "There's a hot bath back here!" I heard her plunge into the water. "Oh, this feels glorious! It's been ages since I had a warm bath. I'm getting all the dirt and grime off me."

"Don't forget the boogers," I said.

Goldie paused for a moment and then said, "Thank you, Red. You're a true friend."

After Goldie had finished washing, the bath was drained and refilled with clean, steaming water for me. I wanted nothing more than to simply collapse on the bed and sleep, but I was horribly dirty, and I knew I'd sleep better if I bathed. Also, I probably didn't smell like roses or anything. I soaked and scrubbed off the dirt and dunked my head beneath the water. I lathered my skin with rose-petal soap.

When I got out of the bath, Goldie was already in bed and fast asleep, her damp curls spread out on her pillow. I dressed in my nightgown, then sat by the fire and dried my hair with a towel. A brush rose from a table of its own accord as though to comb through my tangles.

"Forget it," I said, and it fell back to its place.

I got into bed, which was soft as feathers and satiny smooth. This room didn't look or feel like a prison. I had been well fed, and I smelled better than I had in . . . probably ever, but all these comforts had a suffocating effect. I would rather rot in a dungeon than be fed and pampered while Granny lay dying. I was so close to saving her. Just outside this castle were The Red Roses, but how could I get them without the beast or his gargoyles attacking me?

Far away, a wolf howled, high and mournful. My heart leapt. I slipped out of bed and ran to the window. I couldn't see him, but it was Wolf, of that I was sure. He was calling to me and mourning at the same time.

Come! he howled. I could feel the sadness in his cry. He felt he had failed me. And I had failed him. Who would protect him now?

I pressed my nose to the windowpane. "I'm safe," I told him. "Keep yourself safe, friend." I tried to send my message to him, but my words came out a whisper.

Sleep did not come easily. I kept spinning the events of the day in my head. The roses. The beast. Granny. I suspected the beast would have let us go if I hadn't mentioned Granny's name. Something about it had sparked his interest, and I wondered if perhaps the beast had imprisoned me here for ransom. He said he wanted something. Something that had been taken from him. What could it be? Whatever it was, it seemed he needed magical help to get it back—Granny's help.

CHAPTER TWENTY-ONE

Prankster Palace

In the morning, I woke to Goldie standing over me. She was so close I yelped and flinched. "Goldie, don't *do* that!"

"Did you know you slobber in your sleep?" asked Goldie. "Mummy calls it slobber-sleep. It's not very lady-like."

"I don't give a pig's snout what your mummy thinks. Didn't she ever tell you it's not very ladylike to stare at people while they're sleeping?"

"You're grumpy in the morning," said Goldie.

I scoffed. "Aren't you a smart one?" I threw one of the feather pillows at her, which she caught and hugged to her stomach.

"I'm hungry."

"Were you planning to eat me?"

"Last night when I said I was hungry, the door swung

open. I keep saying it over and over again, but the door won't open this time. I tried to go out the door, but it's locked, just like last night. I don't think anything will happen until we're both awake, so wake up."

I groaned, rolled over, and flopped out of bed. The door stayed shut, but as soon as I was on my feet, a bell rang on the other side of the room, next to a little door in the wall. Goldie opened the tiny door.

"Breakfast!" She lifted a tray with bowls of porridge drizzled with cream and—

"Honey!" cried Goldie, sniffing the sweet scent. There were also fresh strawberries, ripe and red and fragrant. The smell made me homesick for Granny.

Goldie scooped up a spoonful and was about to shove it into her mouth when I knocked it away.

"Hey! What did you do that for?"

"We're prisoners, remember? It could be poisoned."

"Our food wasn't poisoned last night," said Goldie.

"Of course it wasn't. The beast was eating that food, and anyway, you can't always tell right away." I sniffed at the porridge. Most poisons left a bitter aftertaste and sometimes had an odor.

"Red, I'm *starving*," Goldie whined.

I lifted the spoon and took just a tiny lick. I smacked my lips and tried to detect anything sour or bitter, but all I tasted was sweet cream, and it awakened my ravenous hunger. My stomach growled. "I guess it's okay."

Goldie dove for her spoon and devoured the porridge. I ate mine almost as quickly, and then we smashed the strawberries in our mouths.

When our bowls had been licked clean, we found that our clothes had been washed and mended and folded in neat piles on the ends of our beds. Once we were fully dressed, the door clicked open.

Beast stood in the doorway, as though he'd been waiting with great anticipation.

"I'm afraid I've made a bit of a mess in the foyer," he said, and he led us to the entryway near the stairs. Muddy paw prints covered the floors, tables, and chairs. A broom, bucket, and mop presented themselves and gathered around Goldie and me.

"Get to work." Beast sang the words with wicked glee, and left us.

"Oh, ghastly goiters, chores are worse than imprisonment," said Goldie.

"Hmph," I said. "A broom can't *make* me clean up." I went to step around the broom, but it shifted to block my path. I stepped the other way, with the same result.

"Cheeky, huh?! But you're still just a pile of sticks!" I backed up and ran to leap over it, but the moment my feet left the ground, the broom swept me back so that I tripped over the pail, which flipped up in the air and landed on my head.

Goldie stifled a giggle. "Are you hurt?"

I lifted the bucket off my head and threw it against the wall. "Curse all cleaning supplies!" The broom bopped me on the head.

Goldie no longer made any effort to hide her giggles. She keeled over laughing and grasped the mop to keep from falling over, but as soon as she touched the handle, the mop sprang into action. Instead of attacking her, it started to glide and spin Goldie like they were dancing at a ball. "Oh, my goodness, Red, this mop is *romantic!*" The mop hopped and twirled, and Goldie giggled with glee, completely lost in the moment. She even started talking to the mop.

"Why, yes, I would love another dance, thank you."

"Oh, you are *such* a fine dancer."

"What's that? *Marry* you? But what would my mummy say? She would not approve of a mop for a son-in-law!"

While Goldie danced with her romantic mop, I wrestled with my fickle and obstinate broom. I chased it in circles, the bucket trailing at my heels so that I tripped over it at every turn. I finally held the broom down long enough to sweep up some of the mess; a moment later, it wrenched itself free and scattered my dirt pile.

"Aaaargh!" I roared. I took an ax from a nearby suit of armor and pressed it against the broom handle like a blade to the throat. "Behave, or I'll chop you up."

The broom functioned in the appropriate manner after that.

Once we swept up the mess, the broom, mop, and bucket surrendered.

"Phew!" said Goldie. "I'm quite fatigued."

I was likewise exhausted and hoped to find a quiet place to rest. No such luck. Beast was waiting for us right outside the doors, a few feathers stuck in his fur.

"I'm such a clumsy-claws," he said. "I had a run-in with the pillows in the sitting room."

The sitting room looked as though it had snowed inside.

For three days, the beast ordered us about. We swept and mopped and scrubbed until it was dusk, and my knees were bruised and my arms were like melted wax.

And the beast was not our only problem. The castle itself was a formidable foe, bursting with spells and enchantments. Whatever the beast ordered, the castle carried it out. The brooms, buckets, dishes, doors, and furniture all worked like taskmasters, until the third day.

Goldie and I had just finished breakfast when the door opened. We walked through, expecting Beast to be there to give us another chore, but he wasn't. So we were wandering through the corridor and down the stairs when we heard a faint thump.

"What was that?" Goldie asked.

"Our next chore, probably," I said. Beast was probably knocking down a wall just so he could make us clean it up.

We opened doors, peeking in various rooms, but they were all empty.

We heard another thump, louder this time, like something had been dropped or thrown against a wall.

"Perhaps someone is trapped," said Goldie.

"Maybe," I said. Whatever it was, my curiosity had been piqued. We followed the sound to a set of tall doors. Muffled grunts and the occasional thump came from the other side. Slowly, I turned the knob, and the door opened.

The room was an enormous library. The walls stretched higher than the tallest trees in The Woods. The ceiling was a dome of glass that flooded the room with light, illuminating thousands upon thousands of books. I never would have believed so many books existed in the entire world.

Beast stood by a bookshelf, tearing through a volume with feverish passion, as though searching for something. When he did not find it, he growled and flung the book to the floor. The book floated up and placed itself on the shelf while the beast moved on to the next. This continued until he noticed Goldie and me.

"What are you doing here?" he growled.

"Look at all these books!" Goldie exclaimed. "I *love* books. Mummy once got me a book with lots of pictures. I looked at it so many times it fell apart." She started to walk along the bookshelves, brushing the spines with her fingertips. "I wish I still had it. I wonder if there are any books with pictures in here, perhaps one with a handsome prince who kisses awake a beautiful princess— Oh!"

A book lifted itself off the shelf and floated to Goldie. She opened it, and sure enough, the pages were full of colorful pictures. "How lovely!" She settled herself on a cushioned chair and engrossed herself in the book. This seemed to soften the beast somewhat.

"And are you fond of reading, Red?" he asked. "Did your granny read you many books?"

"Books are rare on The Mountain," I said. "Granny mostly told me stories." I had learned my letters and words by reading Granny's spells and potion recipes.

"I will tell you a story, then," said Beast, "one your granny surely never told you." I fiddled with my dress, trying to seem uninterested, but I had a queasy feeling in my stomach that whatever story the beast was about to tell was significant.

"There once was a princess," Beast began, "who had everything she could ever wish for. Gold and silver, land and loyal subjects. She was lively and intelligent. She played instruments and sang sonnets, but above all, she was beautiful, and the fame of her beauty spread throughout the land. Brave knights and handsome princes came from far and wide to win her hand in marriage, and yet the princess was unhappy, for she knew that one day it would all come to an end. She would grow old, and her beauty would fade. Eventually she would die. Oh, the thought was unbearable, that she should grow old and become nothing but bones and dirt in the ground."

I grumbled a little. I didn't need another lecture from a nonhuman about the foolishness of humans despising death. I was sure beasts lived for a thousand years, like dwarves.

The beast continued. "The princess knew of an enchantress rumored to wield powerful magic. The enchantress healed the sick. She gave barren women children and caused failed crops to grow again. The princess summoned the enchantress to her castle and commanded that she make her immortal. She offered her riches. Gold, silver, jewels, half her kingdom, if only she would help her stay young forever. The enchantress refused. It was a foolish idea, she said, and she would have no part in it.

"The princess was not accustomed to being denied, especially in such an insulting manner, so she threatened the enchantress with dungeons and torture and death if she did not obey her command.

"The enchantress laughed. She did not fear such a threat.

"Then the princess did something she had never done in her life. She begged. She got down on her knees and pleaded with the enchantress. She would do anything, anything at all, if only she could live on, forever young and beautiful.

"The enchantress gave a final warning: 'No human should live forever. It goes against human nature.'

" 'Then I don't want to be human!' declared the princess. 'I am more than human! I am royal! Take death away from me!'

" 'If you truly wish it,' said the enchantress. 'I gave you fair warning, but because you are such a determined fool, perhaps you deserve to get your wish.'

"The enchantress spoke an incantation, causing roses to grow in the palace garden. She covered the entire grounds with roses. They crawled over the gates and the statues, overtook the shrubs and trees, and in the center of it all was an enchanted rosebush. Red roses. Magic roses.

" 'Pick one,' said the enchantress. 'Prick your finger on a thorn. Give your blood to the earth, and you shall never die.'

"In eager haste, the princess plucked a rose and pricked her finger. She allowed a drop of her blood to soak into the earth. She felt the magic rush into her body like fire, making her strong, powerful, unbreakable. She was immortal! She danced among the roses until she frightened the gardener, who had been trying vigorously to trim them back. When he saw the princess, he screamed and ran away.

"He is stunned by my immortal beauty, the princess thought.

"She walked through the castle and everyone who saw her fled. The cook, the butler, her ladies-in-waiting. Even soldiers with spears and swords shouted in fear and fled the castle grounds.

"The princess went to her chambers to observe her new immortal state in the mirror, and when she saw herself, she wished to die. She was immortal indeed, but she was no longer human. She was . . ."

"A beast," I whispered. Beast fell quiet. "You're the princess."

"Was," said the beast.

"Wait, *you're* a princess?" said Goldie, dropping her book. "But you're so . . . so . . . you're so . . ."

"Furry? Smelly? Hideous?" snarled the beast.

"I was going to say 'tall,'" said Goldie. "You're very tall for a girl. That's all."

I was still taking this all in. The Red Roses had turned the princess into a beast. A beast that could live forever. I pressed my face into my hands. I could have turned Granny into a beast. If it weren't for the gargoyles, I could have turned myself into a beast. And now I could see all the regret in the eyes of this princess-beast—regret that she had ever wished for immortality.

"Did the enchantress tell you how you might break the curse?" I asked.

The beast shook her head. "It's impossible," she said bitterly.

"Oh, no," I said. "Every curse has a means of escape,

even if you don't know it. I have a friend who was cursed since birth, and he had no idea how to break it, but he still did."

"I never said I didn't know the way. I said it was impossible."

"If there's a way to break it, then it is possible," I said.

"Oh! Oh!" shouted Goldie, waving her arms around like a lunatic. "I know what it is! True love's kiss! Mummy told me a story once of a princess under a spell, but the spell was broken by true love's kiss!"

"That's a lovely story," said Beast, "but this spell will not be broken by true love's kiss."

"If you were a prince, I'd kiss you right now," said Goldie. "Then I'd be a princess and Mummy would love me for certain." Goldie puckered up as though she truly thought to kiss the beast.

"But she's not a prince," I said, restraining Goldie. "She's a princess. Or was."

Beast had backed up against a bookshelf, as if she thought the threat of Goldie's kiss was real.

"It doesn't matter," said the beast. "I can't break the spell, and I'll be a beast forever."

I drummed my fingers on a stack of books, thinking. If Granny were here, she'd know what to do. I'd seen her help others in similar predicaments, though perhaps nothing quite so extreme. Obviously the roses didn't interest me anymore, but perhaps I could barter with Beast, convince her to release us in exchange for Granny's magical advice.

"I think I know someone who might be able to help you," I said.

"Yes," said the beast. "I know. In fact, that is precisely why you are here."

I nodded, my suspicions now confirmed. Granny wouldn't be able to break the curse for Beast, or change her back to a princess, but she could tell her if she would ever break the spell, and perhaps give her a few clues as to how. It might be my only chance of escape.

"My granny knows a lot about magic," I said. "If you release us, I can take you to her. She's very ill, but she'd still help you find a way to break your curse."

The beast stared at me for a moment, something like laughter in her eyes, though I couldn't see what was so funny. "That won't be necessary," she said. "I've already sent word to your granny."

"I don't understand."

The beast turned away from me and brushed her claws along the books, leaving scratch marks on the spines. I could almost feel the books cringing in pain. "Enchantress . . . ," said Beast. "It's just a nice name for a witch, you know. A witch did this to me, and now I hold the key to making her change me back—her one and only grandchild."

I gaped at Beast. The realization crept over me, cold and slow, like frost on a windowpane. "You mean . . ."

The beast nodded. "Rose Red the Enchantress, or as people now call her, The Witch of The Woods."

CHAPTER TWENTY-TWO
Beastly Destiny

Granny. Rose Red. The enchantress who transformed a princess into a beast. She had never told me this story before. I guess I could see why. It wasn't something to be proud of, transforming a princess into a beast, even if the princess *had* demanded it. It was a cruel fate and I understood why the beast had made us her prisoners, but she obviously didn't understand that kidnapping me was a useless ploy.

"She won't undo the curse," I said.

"She will if she wants to see her only grandchild."

"You can't keep us here forever!" said Goldie.

"Has your affection for me died so soon?"

Goldie cowered, clutching her book of handsome princes and fair princesses to her chest.

"You don't understand," I said. "She *can't* undo the curse, even if she were well enough. She doesn't have the power. Curses can't be reversed or undone, only broken, according to whatever rules were set forth at the time of the cursing, so the only way—"

The beast roared, causing books to tumble from shelves. "I know the rules! Now I'm setting *my* rules! Your granny will turn me back into a princess or she will die knowing that you are in my power."

"And at the end of it all, you'll *still* be a beast!" I shouted.

The beast's hairy brow furrowed ever so slightly. I thought she was about to cry, her sapphire-blue eyes glistened so, but then she roared and raked her claws over another row of books so that they crashed to the floor. She burst through the doors and ran away on all fours.

The library busied itself, picking up the books the beast had displaced, stacking them neatly on the shelves.

"Red, do you think we'll ever go home?" Goldie asked.

I closed my eyes. It was my fault Goldie was here. I had gotten her into this mess. "We'll find a way out, Goldie," I said. "I promise."

A book suddenly lifted off a shelf and dropped onto my head.

"Ouch! What was that for?" I picked up the book and read the title.

The Broken Promise.

I hurled it across the room, but it simply floated back up to the shelf and slid itself neatly into place. Magic books. They won't even let you get properly enraged.

Why hadn't Granny told me about the beast? Was she ashamed? Had she truly meant to turn the princess into a beast, or had it been a disastrous magical mistake? I had never imagined Granny made any mistakes with magic, but clearly I didn't know everything about Granny.

"It's a good thing you didn't get one of The Red Roses," said Goldie. "Otherwise, you might have turned your granny into a beast!"

"I suppose so," I said, though I wondered if the spell might work differently if you didn't want it for yourself, but for someone else. Granny said that selfishness was one of the reasons magic always went wrong. But I didn't want eternal life for myself. I wanted it for Granny. That wasn't selfish, was it?

"What about that other magic . . . ?" Goldie mused while turning the pages of another book. "The Magic Hearts. I told you to try that from the beginning. It sounds nice."

I had pushed it out of mind because the dwarves knew so little of it. "I don't even know what a Magic Heart is or where to find one," I said.

"Maybe it's something you find in your own heart?" guessed Goldie.

"That doesn't even make sense," I said. "I need to figure out how the magic works."

I knew The Magic Hearts existed. The dwarves said so. I just needed more information. Granny always says the best way to gain knowledge is through your own experience. The second-best way is to learn from others. Stories. Lessons. Books.

Books! Here I was in a place full of information, and all I had to do was ask.

"Goldie," I said. "We can ask the library about Magic Hearts!"

"Goodness, why didn't I think of that? Here, let me ask." She closed her book and stood up. "Oh, library, wilt thou give us a book about The Magic Hearts?"

Nothing happened at first, and then a book removed itself from a low shelf and floated toward us. I took it and eagerly read the pages, with Goldie peering over my shoulder, but I was disappointed in the story. It was a tale about a girl who gave her heart to a boy, but he threw it away. Where her heart lay there grew a willow tree called The Wishing Willow, and anyone who wished for true love beneath that tree would find it.

"That was the saddest, most beautiful story in the world!" Goldie sniffled.

"But it's not helpful." I shut the book and pushed it back toward the shelf. "I need a book that will tell me how to stop death."

The library brought down another book full of remedies for common illnesses, but nothing out of the ordinary.

"Oh, gross," said Goldie. "There's the recipe for the tonic Mummy always makes me drink!" She made a gagging noise and tossed the book back to the shelf.

"We might have more luck if we search separately," I said.

"Good idea," said Goldie. "I'll go ask the other side of the library. You stay here and keep asking this side. We'll find something!"

I asked about Magic Hearts in a dozen different ways, and the library brought down book after book. I read stories and histories and remedies, each having something to do with hearts, magic, or forever, but none brought me any closer to knowing how I might save Granny.

Across the library, I could hear Goldie's requests and then her subsequent reactions to whatever book the library had given her. She giggled, gasped, and sobbed, while I grumbled and growled at my fruitless search. In a library with this many books, there had to be something useful.

"Can't you find *any* book that mentions Magic Hearts? Just Magic Hearts so a person will never die." The words came out a little snippety, so I added, "Please."

The library was still for a minute, like it was thinking or searching for the right book. Finally another book came down to me from the very tallest shelf. It was old and worn. It looked promising. I settled into a big chair and opened the pages. At first glance, I thought it was a spell book and my heart leapt, but it turned out to be nothing more than nursery rhymes, all rather silly and nonsensical.

I slammed it shut and started to fling it back when something caught my eye. A page hung out of the book, torn from the binding. Two words jumped out at me: "never" and "die."

I opened the book to a rhyme called "Hearts of the Huntsman." It felt odd compared to the others, mysterious and melancholy. Each verse was a tragic tale of how someone died, whether by illness, accident, or old age, but at the end of three sad verses was this stanza:

> *Who will o'erthrow Death*
> *That man may keep his breath?*
> *What pow'rs be in the land*
> *To stay Death's chilling hand?*
> *The old huntsman knows*

How the Hearts grow
The Magic for those
Who wish never to die

"Goldie, come look at this."

Goldie read the poem, her eyebrows knit in concentration. "The old huntsman knows . . ." She traced her finger over the line.

"Do you think maybe Horst could know something?" I asked.

"Well, he's certainly old," said Goldie.

"And see how it mentions 'Hearts' and 'Magic,' as though they mean something more." I'd been trying to stay as far away from Horst as possible in order to protect Wolf, but maybe he held the answers I sought. Had I been wrong to refuse his help?

It didn't matter. Unless we could escape the castle, there was no point to any of it, especially if Granny was . . .

No. I wouldn't think of that. I refused. Mama and Papa should be home soon. They could be home now and they would surely go right to Granny's. She would be fine. At least for now. Granny and I were so connected that I believed I would feel it if she were gone, like a bone breaking. Surely she was holding on for me.

🐾

The beast did not dine with us that evening, nor the next. She issued no orders, made no demands. She didn't even show herself, which made me feel uneasy.

With no Beast to boss us about, Goldie and I were left to the care of the castle. It gave us the freedom to wander around, though it kept us locked inside.

I could not enjoy the freedom. I couldn't stop thinking about the terrible fate Granny had bestowed upon Beast. I couldn't stop worrying about Granny and Wolf. I couldn't stop wondering about The Magic Hearts, and what Horst might have to do with them.

I lay in bed that night, Goldie snoring next to me. I slept with my cloak, and I fingered the corners anxiously, trying to draw comfort, wisdom, hope.

Wolf howled.

Come back, he said, and I sensed his growing urgency. Was he in danger? Was Horst coming after him? It felt like we were both running out of time. His cries had lulled me to sleep these past nights, but tonight they kept me awake.

Another howl sounded, but this one was nearer, inside the castle.

Beast.

I sat up. A candle lit on my bedside. I took it and went to the door. I pressed my hand against it.

The door unlocked and opened.

The sconces lit up along the wall as I traveled down the corridor, down the staircase.

The terrible howling came again. There was no meaning to it, except despair. I wandered through the castle aimlessly, but then I saw the shadow of Beast cross the corridor. I blew out my candle and silently followed. She walked through a maze of rooms and hallways, until she came to the library. She entered and shut the door.

What was she doing in the library in the middle of the night? Reading bedtime stories?

I turned the knob and slowly pushed the door open, just enough to peer through with one eye.

Beast stood in front of a bookshelf, casting long, ghoulish shadows across the room. She reached for a book, but when she lifted it, there was a click, and a portion of the shelf swung open, revealing a corridor behind. Beast slipped inside, and the shelf closed behind her, leaving me in darkness.

I should have just gone back to bed. But I couldn't help myself. I was curious to know where Beast was going and what she was doing.

Curiosity killed the cat, said a small voice in my head. It sounded eerily like Granny's.

But I'm not a cat, I said back to the voice. Besides, this was my captor, whom I wished to escape, so it made sense that I should follow her and find out all I could. I walked to the shelf and felt along the spines of the books. Beast had reached for a book at the level of her chest, which meant it would be above my head. I tipped a book back as I had seen Beast do, but nothing happened. I pulled more books, working my way along the shelf. One or two fell down, but they quickly picked themselves up and floated back onto the shelves. I clutched another book and tugged. This one felt different, like it was attached to something. I pulled until something snapped, then I released the book and the shelf swung open.

CHAPTER TWENTY-THREE

The Beauty in the Mirror

Through the opening in the bookshelf, I found myself in a hallway with a door at the other end. I was certain it would be locked, but when I turned the knob, it swung open on silent hinges. I stepped into a vast hall. Endless. It stretched for ages in both directions, and there were people all around, all of them covered in red cloaks. I stared at them, and they stared back, until I realized it was only me. Hundreds of Reds staring at herself. The walls were covered floor to ceiling with mirrors.

I didn't see Beast anywhere. Granny always says never to trust mirrors. They can be tricky things, especially if they've been enchanted, which I suspected these were. Some mirrors will reflect things as they really are, while others reflect things that could be, or things that are happening elsewhere, or even things that you wished were true.

I saw myself reflected in the mirror dozens of times. Just plain Red. Same tangle of brown hair, sharp gray eyes, and small pale face.

Something shifted in the nearest mirror to my right. A woman appeared. A real beauty. Her skin was flawless, a hint of pink in her cheeks and on her lips. Her sapphire-blue eyes contrasted sharply with chestnut hair that curled softly around her face and shoulders. She looked familiar to me, but it was impossible that I had seen her before now.

"Her name is Beauty," said a voice. The woman's lips moved like she was speaking, but the voice was far too deep to belong to her. I turned and found Beast standing in front of the beautiful woman in the mirror.

"The name suits her," I said.

"Do you think so?" said Beast. "I'm not so certain."

"What do you mean?" I said. "No one would deny that she's beautiful."

"I believe many would deny it," said Beast. "Especially now."

I looked back and forth between the beast and the girl in the mirror. There was no resemblance, except for the striking similarity of their eyes.

"She's you," I said. "This is you before . . ."

"Before I asked your grandmother for immortality," said Beast. "Yes. This was me. My name was Beauty."

"It still is," I said. "A name can't be taken away."

"Yes, a great load of good it's doing me now, isn't it?" she said wryly.

I looked down at my feet. Though we say your name is your destiny, and parents choose names carefully, it's not a guarantee for a happily-ever-after. Mistakes can be made, tragedy can occur, and other people's destinies can get tangled with your own and make a mess. I'd gotten tangled up in such messes before, and now I was dishing them out right and left. Goldie, Borlen, Wolf . . . maybe even Beast.

Beast stared at her former beautiful self with longing. I wondered how many hours she spent here, just wishing to be beautiful again.

Something moved in a mirror to my left, a shadow shifting in a thick forest. It was hazy and far away, so I couldn't tell what it was.

Beast cleared her throat. "I received a message from your granny."

I whipped around and faced Beast. "You did? When? How is she?" My heart ballooned with hope.

"She's alive. She hoped the castle was feeding you well and asked me to remind you to wash behind your ears."

"That's all?" My heart deflated.

"She gave me a message, too. She told me to take a look in the mirror and remember."

"Remember what?" I asked.

"How to break the curse."

I gaped. "She *told* you how to break the curse?" Granny never *told* someone how to break a curse. She skirted, hinted, and teased, but never would she tell you exactly what to do. "What did she say?"

"She said, 'Love life more than you fear death.'"

I frowned. "That's it? All you have to do is love life?"

"More than I fear death."

"But how can you control that? How can anyone *choose* not to be afraid?"

"If I knew, I would not look like this," said Beast. "And if you knew, you would not be here, would you?"

I looked down at my cloak and rubbed the edges between my fingers, then glanced back to the mirror where the beast was reflected as Beauty. I understood her a little better now. How could she love life as a beast? And how could she not fear death as Beauty? It seemed upside down and inside out, and I was having difficulty not resenting Granny at that moment.

I turned away from Beast's beautiful reflection, and a movement caught my gaze. In the other mirror, shadows came together and took the shape of a figure. But Beast paid no attention to it.

"It is a hard thing to lose someone you love," said Beast. "But perhaps the harder thing to lose is yourself." Beast looked back in the mirror at her beautiful reflection. "We lose ourselves when we're afraid."

"Is that why you asked Granny to make you live forever?" I asked. "Because you were afraid?"

"I am still afraid," said Beast. "But I've learned at least one thing."

"What?" I asked.

"Life is like a story. It doesn't mean anything if it doesn't end."

My heart squeezed in my chest, for this felt true to me, however painful. It's not that I needed Granny to live forever. I just couldn't imagine a time when I wouldn't need her.

"If I could just . . ." But the words swelled in my throat. My eyes burned.

Beast put a gentle paw on my shoulder and turned me toward her. I looked up into her furry face, so monstrous, and yet somehow softer and kinder than many human faces I'd seen. "I am what I am because I was afraid."

I dried the traitorous tears running down my cheeks. "You're not so bad," I said. "I've met uglier humans, at least on the inside."

"Humans can be pretty beastly, can't they?"

I nodded. Funny that we always tell stories with wolves and beasts and demons as villains, but in real life it seems the humans are always the worst enemies. You could be your own villain.

"I know you want Granny to turn you back into a princess, but she can't. Truly." I said the words gently, without rage or malice.

Beast nodded, resigned to the truth, but no happier about it.

"You'll find a way to break the curse yourself," I said. "Granny must have known that. She would never have cast a spell that would have truly cursed you forever."

Beast nodded. "Your granny seems to be a very wise witch."

"She is."

"And because she is so wise, she will not live forever."

I looked away. My throat tightened, so I couldn't speak. Though I knew Beast was right, I still couldn't look the truth directly in the eye.

"She will want to see you strong," said Beast. "Before it's too late."

I looked up. "You mean we can go?"

Beast nodded. "Keeping you won't do me any good. At least, it won't change anything."

But I did see a glimmer of change in her, just a small ray of hope that the curse would be broken one day, somehow. I thought Granny would be proud of Beast in that moment.

"Thank you, Beauty," I said, and turned to leave.

"Red?" said Beast.

"Yes?" I said, turning back.

"Don't be afraid."

I heard Granny's words echoing in my head.

Don't be afraid, Red.

She had said it when I first tried to use the magic inside me. She said it when I was leaving to try to find a cure for her.

Red, don't be afraid.

I so wanted to be brave, truly brave, not just strong and fierce. I thought I was beginning to know how.

"Red!" I heard Goldie shouting from outside the room. She sounded frantic. I ran to the door, and she came barreling through, panting. "Where have you been? I woke up and you were gone and I was hungry and the room wouldn't give me any food and who are all these people?" She gaped at the hundreds of Beauties and Reds and Goldies reflected in all the mirrors.

"It's okay, Goldie. They're just mirrors."

"My hair is an awful mess," she said.

Beast chuckled, probably thinking how she wouldn't mind messy hair instead of all her fur.

"Goldie, we can go home now," I said.

Her eyes widened. "We can?" She looked from me to Beast. We both nodded.

"Is your granny going to break the curse, then? Will she be a princess again?"

"Not yet," I said. I looked back to the mirror where the image of Beauty was now turned toward us.

"Who's that?" Goldie pointed.

"Her name is Beauty," I said.

"Not her. The person next to her."

I shifted my gaze. The other figure in the mirror was much closer now. He was out of The Woods and walking through the rose garden, seemingly walking right toward the mirror. The figure had a stiff gait and was covered with what looked like furs, with a bow and quiver of arrows slung over his shoulder. "It's Horst," I said.

"Where is he? Can he see us?" Goldie asked.

Horst came closer and closer, so close that if he walked any farther, he'd walk straight through the mirror. But he stopped just behind Beast's beautiful reflection and squinted his old eyes as though searching for something. Beast growled a little at Horst's image.

"Do you know him?" I asked Beast.

Beast did not answer. Horst nocked an arrow, pointing it straight at Beast. She stared at the hunter in the mirror, frozen like a poor animal caught in a trap.

Horst released the arrow. The mirror shattered, bits

and shards of glass exploding in every direction. I grabbed Goldie and pulled her into the protection of my cloak. Beast roared. When the glass settled, I looked up. Beast had an arrow in her leg.

And there was Horst, standing amidst the shattered glass, his face stony and unreadable. Without a word, he grabbed another arrow and shot Beast in the other leg. She roared again and collapsed to her front paws.

"No!" I shouted at Horst, punching him as hard as I could, which hurt my hand quite a bit and Horst not at all. His stomach was as hard as rock. He looked down at me as though I were a harmless bug, until something big and solid crashed into another mirror. A gargoyle. Another came down, and another. They snarled and lunged at Horst, but Horst didn't even flinch at the stone monsters. He punched one directly in the face, crushing the stone as though it were brittle bone. Another attacked him from behind, but Horst grabbed it and threw it across the room.

Beast had now pulled the arrows out of her legs and was struggling to stand. Horst nocked another arrow.

"Stop! Stop! Don't hurt her!" Goldie cried.

I moved to attack Horst at the same time as a gargoyle. Its stone wing clipped me on the back of my head, swift and hard. I stumbled back. The room went bright. It spun and shattered like the broken mirror, and then all went black.

CHAPTER TWENTY-FOUR

Where the Heart Is

I woke in a dimly lit room with a wolf staring down at me. I sat up quickly and then cried out as my head exploded.

"You're awake!" Goldie jumped to my side. "She's awake!" she said to someone else.

"Careful," said a gruff voice. "That gargoyle smacked you good and hard. You're going to have to take it easy."

Horst stood beside me, holding a steaming cup. I took a sip and immediately spat it out. It was horribly bitter.

"Drink it," said Horst. "It will help with the pain."

I drank two big gulps, and the pain did ease a bit. My head became clear enough to remember that I had seen a wolf. I looked up. Its head was mounted to the wall.

I swallowed my own scream. *It's all right. It's okay. This is the huntsman's home, after all.*

The walls were covered with the skins and heads of every sort of beast of The Woods. Deer, moose, bears, mountain lions, jackrabbits, and wolves. I counted six wolves on the wall, teeth bared, with shiny black stones for eyes. Was this Wolf's pack, hunted and hung on a wall? My heart ached for Wolf. I trembled and clutched the blanket in my fists, only to feel that it was also fur. The hair was brown and matted. It reminded me of Beast. I flung it off me.

"You shot Beast!" I shouted at Horst. "You killed her!" I lunged at Horst, but the room spun and I collapsed back on the bed.

"Easy there," said Horst. "I promise you, Miss Red, I didn't kill the beast. Injured her, perhaps, but she'll heal soon enough and live to be a beast for another thousand years, cursed as she is."

I closed my eyes and breathed until the room was still again. Horst was right. Beast couldn't be killed, no matter what. The arrow and the shattered glass had made me panic and forget that Beast could not die. She didn't need my help.

"Then . . . you know about Beast's curse?" I asked.

Horst nodded.

"How did you know Beast was holding us prisoner?" I asked.

Horst seemed caught off guard by the question. "Your granny . . . She told me a beast was holding you captive. She asked me to rescue you. She couldn't in her condition, of course."

This didn't sound like Granny. She firmly believed people should rescue themselves, but then, she was ill, possibly out of her mind, and I was her only grandchild.

"I have to get to Granny," I said, trying to stand up again, but Horst restrained me.

"Hold on there, little Red. Not so fast. That gargoyle gave you a right nasty smack in the head."

"Did you see him fight the gargoyles?" Goldie asked. "He ripped off one of their arms like an ear of corn!"

Horst smiled. "I have a good amount of strength when the situation calls for it."

"We were fine," I said. "Beast was letting us go when you came."

"Well, she shouldn't have taken you in the first place. What a horrible thing to do to two little girls."

Yes, it had been horrible at first, but the beast wasn't so bad in the end. Funny how that works. Sometimes things in life seem okay in the beginning but then turn out to be horrible. The problem is, you can't really know until it's too late.

Horst put more wood on the fire.

"I'm hungry," said Goldie. "At the castle, we'd be having breakfast now."

Horst took out some dried meat from his satchel and handed us each a piece, taking none for himself. Goldie stared at the shriveled jerky. "At the castle, we would have had porridge with honey," she said.

"Well, I don't have any honey," said Horst, a slight edge to his voice. We ate the meat. It was tough and salty. We could barely tear through it with our back teeth, but after looking at all the animals on the walls, I didn't much care to eat anyway.

"Now," said Horst when Goldie had given up on her leathery meal, "something tells me you didn't end up at the enchanted castle by accident. You were looking for something, weren't you? Perhaps some roses?"

I glanced at Goldie.

"I told him you were trying to save your granny," said Goldie. "He already knew about The Red Roses."

I shifted, uncomfortable under Horst's intense gaze.

"You failed to retrieve the roses, but I think I may have what you're looking for," said Horst. I thought of the rhyme I had found in Beast's library, but I felt uneasy. The wolves on the wall seemed to call to me, warning me to leave.

Go, they said.

"I really need to get home to Granny," I said. "I think I can walk just fine now."

"But don't you want to save your granny?" Horst asked. "Your friend said she was dying. If there was a way to save her, to keep her from death, wouldn't you want to know?"

I thought back on my journey. The Wine Well. The Red Roses. So far, each magic had come at too high a price. But there was one magic left that I had not fully explored. What if it really could save Granny? Should I turn my back on one last chance?

"Do you know anything about Magic Hearts?" I asked.

Horst smiled a little. "It sounds familiar. I will share my secrets, but in return, I need to know yours."

"I don't have any secrets," I said.

"Oh, everyone has secrets, and I believe little witches have the best secrets of all, don't you agree?" Horst's eyes were dark and glassy in the dim light. They looked hungry.

"Let me tell you a story," Horst said.

"Does it have a princess in it?" Goldie asked. "I only like stories with princesses."

"It does indeed." Horst cleared his throat and leaned forward in his chair. It reminded me of when Beast had told me her story in the library, but it was different. A chill crept up my arms as I listened to Horst, like a spider creeping slowly up my arm.

"Once upon a time," said the huntsman, "an evil queen ruled The Kingdom. She was jealous of her step-child, the princess Snow White."

Goldie sighed with exasperation. "Not that one! We've all heard it a thousand times. The queen tries to kill Snow White, so she goes to live with dwarves, and then the queen tries to kill her again with a poisoned apple, but then a prince comes along and kisses her awake."

"Yes," said Horst, looking slightly annoyed. "That is one version of the story. I'm going to tell you another. Now, before the poisoned apple, the queen ordered a huntsman to take the girl deep into The Woods and kill her. He was told to bring the girl's heart as proof of her death."

The hair at the nape of my neck prickled. Huntsman. A heart. Horst couldn't possibly have been that hunts-man. The story was over a hundred years old.

"But he didn't kill the princess," said Goldie.

"No," said Horst. "The huntsman had killed many a beast in his lifetime, but he could not bear to kill such an innocent child, so he let her go, and then he killed a boar and took its heart to the queen and told her it was the heart of the princess. The queen intended to eat the heart for her victory feast. However, the queen, being greedy and vain, wanted to hear straightaway from her magic mirror that she was the fairest in all The Kingdom. But the mirror revealed that the princess Snow White was still alive. 'Not so,' said the queen. 'For here I have proof of her death. Her heart!' But the mirror had seen everything and told the queen how the huntsman had deceived her. Faster than he could draw an arrow, he was seized and thrown into the dungeon."

"The poor man!" said Goldie. "It's so unfair."

"For days, the queen gave the huntsman no food or water. He was on the brink of death, barely able to move, when finally she came to him.

" 'Please,' said the huntsman. He reached his hand toward the queen, begging her to save him. The queen gave him no bread or water but placed in his hand the boar's heart he had brought to her instead of Snow White's.

" 'This will be your last supper, huntsman,' said the queen, and she left him, never to return again.

"The huntsman clutched that heart to his chest and waited to die. Except he did not die. The huntsman stayed alive for weeks and months. There was no food or water, nothing in his cell except the heart. After several months, he realized it was the heart, still clutched tightly to his chest, that kept him alive. And not only did it keep him alive, it made him strong, so strong that he dug himself out of the dungeon. He clawed through the stone, dug through the dirt, until he reached the outside world. Free! Alive! And famished. He became suddenly weak and tired. His joints stiffened. His muscles seized. He knew that whatever magic the heart had given him was now fading. He needed more.

"So he took the heart of another boar, and his power was restored. He took other hearts, too. Goats, sheep, deer, even bears, mountain lions, and wolves. Each beast made him stronger. And with his many hearts, the huntsman lived happily ever after.

"The end."

Horst sat back, a sadistic grin on his face. Goldie looked at me, her mouth open in horror. This was not what I had expected. I had assumed The Magic Hearts had something to do with love. *The best magic comes from the heart.* But according to Horst's story, they were actual *hearts.* That's what Horst carried in the pouch hung around his neck—the heart of whatever beast was giving him his power. He was tugging at it now, staring at me, and I knew what he wanted.

The wolves on the wall howled for me to go. *Leave. Run.*

"That wasn't a very good story," said Goldie, apparently unaware of the truth of Horst's tale.

"You don't think so?" Horst seemed amused.

Goldie shook her head. "There wasn't even a true love's kiss."

Horst scoffed. "True love. Perhaps that's all fine and

well for brave knights and fair damsels, but what about the rest of us? You could live a lifetime and never find true love. I've seen it over and over. And even if you do find love, what then? It's not as powerful as the stories always say. Is true love going to keep you alive? Will it make you strong? No."

"Yes!" said Goldie. "When I find true love, it will!"

Horst shook his head. "Love cannot give you power. *Living.* Defying death. That's power."

"And you hold that power, don't you?" I blurted. "You're the huntsman in the story, and those are your Magic Hearts." I gestured to the pouch around his neck.

Horst smiled. "Clever girl."

Goldie looked between us. "Wait. You mean *you're* the one who almost killed Snow White? But . . . that happened hundreds of years ago!"

"Two hundred and twenty-three years, to be precise."

"You took Granny's pigs," I spat. "For their hearts. And the wolves . . ." I gritted my teeth. "You killed Wolf's pack." Everything was coming into sharp focus. Why hadn't I seen this all before? His age, his pitiful, bumbling slowness, had pulled the wool over my eyes, kept me from seeing what he really was.

"Come now," said Horst. "You don't think those vicious wolves would have done the same to me, given the chance? And I needed those pigs. I daresay they would have met the same end without me."

"You're a huntsman, aren't you? Seems awfully cowardly to hunt helpless pigs in a pen."

Horst's composure faltered ever so slightly. "The

animals . . . they've become aware of me. They hide and flee before I can catch them, and poor old Horst must have something."

I thought of how still and silent The Woods had been at times along our journey—when Horst was near. It was meaningless to me then, but I understood it now. It was as if they could sense the sinister magic in Horst, his brutal intentions, and now I could feel it, too, crawling all over my arms and neck like spiders.

"And now," said Horst, "let's talk about your friend, the wolf. I'd like a word with him."

"Friend?" I said, forcing a laugh. "Wolves are very dangerous creatures. I don't see how I can help you."

"You're not fooling me," said Horst. "Your little friend Goldie told me all about it, how the wolf trusts you, how he follows you around like a puppy."

Goldie was shaking her head, tears springing to her eyes. "I'm sorry, Red! I didn't know! I didn't know he was so horrible! I thought he'd understand."

"Indeed, I do!" said Horst. "I understand better than anyone. You wish to keep your grandmother alive, and I have the same wish for myself. What do you say, little Red? Shall we go for a walk? Shall we meet a wolf? They are particularly valuable to me."

"You've said that before. Why? Why are they *particularly* valuable?"

"It has to do with the magic inside the heart, you see," said Horst. "The more powerful the animal, the more powerful the heart, the longer it keeps me going. A moose gives me a solid month. A mountain lion, two, and one bear heart can keep me going for nearly three. But wolves . . ." Horst looked directly at me. "Wolves are the real prize. Wolves can keep me going for *years*."

"Then you should be safe for quite a while," I said, glancing at the wolf heads on the walls, their dead eyes so cold and empty.

"Ah, but that's the interesting thing about wolves. Wolves are social creatures, unified and loyal. That's where their magic comes from. Their hearts work as one, as a pack. In order to get the magic from one, I need them all, and once I have them all, it might just be enough magic to share with someone else. Someone very sick, nearly dying . . ."

My blood ran cold. I shook my head.

"I can save your granny," said Horst. "Keep her from dying for a long, long time, maybe even forever. *You* could live forever, too."

Eternal life. It sounded like good magic. Anything that makes you live and grow is good, right? But the hearts . . . though they kept Horst alive, I didn't think they made him grow and blossom, as Granny said good magic should. He was twisted and corrupt—cursed, maybe more so than Beast. Granny would never wish for such a fate. She wouldn't even consider it.

"I can't help you," I said.

Horst's face fell. "What will you do when she dies? Who will you have then?"

"She has me!" shouted Goldie. "I'm her dearest friend in all the world."

Horst sighed. "Well then, I suppose there's only one

thing to be done." He pulled out his long, curved knife. It flashed in the firelight. I flinched, but Horst didn't touch me. He grabbed a handful of Goldie's curls.

"Ouch! That hurts, you horrible, mean man!"

"What would you do for your dearest friend in all the world?" said Horst. "Would you help *me* to save *her*?"

"Let her go," I said in a weak voice.

"Red, don't help him! I'm not afraid to die! I'm noooaaagh!" Horst yanked cruelly on her hair, but Goldie grasped the poker by the fire, glowing hot, and waved it around until it smacked Horst on the head. He hollered and dropped his knife, slapping at his smoking hair.

"Run, Red!" Goldie grabbed my hand and we raced to the door. I burst through, practically breaking it off its hinges, and both Goldie and I tumbled outside. I grabbed Goldie's hand and yanked her to her feet, then shoved her down again as Horst let loose an arrow. It came right at me, but I lifted my cloak and the arrow fell harmlessly to the ground.

I glanced back at Horst. He reached for another arrow, his face set with grim determination.

"Stay inside my cloak," I whispered to Goldie. She nodded, and we rose together and ran into The Woods. Horst shot at us again and again. The arrows whistled past my ears and pierced the trees. We were slow and awkward, two girls huddled together, hobbling through a dark forest, but Horst couldn't be much faster. His hearts had made him strong and powerful, but stiff and slow, too. There had to be consequences for such magic. Maybe even more than Horst realized.

Soon we outdistanced him. The arrows stopped, and I heard no footsteps in pursuit. We slowed to a walk.

"Do you know where we are?" Goldie asked.

I shook my head. We were in The Woods—near home—but our surroundings were dark and unfamiliar to me. I had no idea where Horst's cabin was in relation to anything else. Were we north of the village? South, east, west? Where was my path? I took a few steps in every direction, hoping it would appear, willing it to life, but nothing happened.

Goldie started to shiver beside me. I didn't think it had to do with cold so much as shock. She'd had one too many frights for a day, but I couldn't afford to give in to fear. I had to get us home.

"Let's keep walking," I said. "We'll find our way."

CHAPTER TWENTY-FIVE

A Red Spell

We walked for what seemed like hours, and still The Woods were unfamiliar. It was eerily silent. No creatures spoke. The nymphs did not whisper their memories, and the trees felt cold and lifeless. The only thing that moved was the mist, spilling over the ground like an overflowing potion, so thick my path would not have been visible even if it did appear.

I pulled my hood over my head and wrapped my cloak tightly around Goldie and myself.

A twig snapped. A flock of birds exploded out of a tree.

Fly! Danger! they cried.

Goldie jumped and clutched my arm. I searched for the cause of alarm. There was movement in the mist. My first instinct was to run, but then I paused. The figure was approaching too fast to be Horst, its movements graceful and agile.

I let out the breath I'd been holding. "It's Wolf."

He bounded up to me and knocked me over. He licked my face and wagged his tail like an excited pup.

I laughed. "Glad to see you, too," I said. I picked myself up and scratched his ruff, feeling his relief, worry, anger, and excitement, all mixed together. He growled, low and fierce.

Monster! he said, and for once I understood. The images of Wolf's pack flashed through my mind, disappearing one by one. I now recognized them as the wolves I had seen adorning Horst's walls.

"I know," I said. "Horst is a monster, but I won't let him hurt you. I promise." Wolf touched his nose to my fingers. I felt his complete trust, and the weight of my promise pressed down heavily upon me.

"Look!" said Goldie, pointing at her feet.

The mist had thinned enough for us to see the faint outline of a path. My path. It seemed to flicker in and out of view, threatening to disappear again, like it was having difficulty breathing.

Granny . . .

Granny had made my path with her magic. If the path was fading, that might mean Granny was, too. . . .

"Let's go," I said. We walked as quickly as we could, and soon our surroundings started to look familiar. The knots in the trees, the rise of a hill, the rocks and brush— these were my Woods, but I did not feel at home.

When we reached Granny's cottage, it did not grow out of the trees with its usual flair and flourish. It just sat there, a dark and lonesome hut. No tendrils of smoke rose from the chimney, no candles glowed through the windows. No pigs or chickens clustered by the fence to greet me.

"It looks a little . . . abandoned," said Goldie.

"That's just because Granny's been ill," I said, my voice catching in my throat. "She's probably sleeping."

Wolf growled a little. He didn't like the looks of it, either.

"Wait here," I said.

"I'll go with you, Red," said Goldie. "You shouldn't be alone."

"It's all right," I said. "Stay here. Granny isn't fond of strangers."

Wolf whined some more and nipped at the edge of my cloak.

Stay.

"I have to go see Granny." I left them behind and approached the cottage. My heart pounded faster and louder with each step. My stomach and throat tightened into knots. Was I too late? In my quest to save Granny, had I missed what little time I had left with her?

Knock, knock, knock. I tapped on the door. "Granny?" I called. "It's Red."

"Come in, child. It's not locked."

I sighed with relief. Granny's voice was very hoarse, but she was here. She was alive.

I opened the door. The house was dim and shadowy,

but the cottage was much as I had left it—bread on the table, vials and jars on the shelves, dried herbs hanging from the ceiling—though it smelled funny. The usual fragrance of herbs and spices was overpowered by the smell of smoke and game. I guessed this was the smell of someone who'd been ill and bedridden, but for some reason it made the hair on my arms prickle. It wasn't the right smell for Granny's cottage.

I looked to the bed and almost laughed. Granny was in her wolf costume! She must have been feeling better if she was in good enough spirits to be playing jokes. She must have known I was coming!

"Oh, Granny, what big eyes you have."

She said nothing. Perhaps she could not hear me. I stepped closer and spoke a little louder.

"Oh, Granny, what big *ears* you have."

Nothing. I stepped closer, my face inches from the wolf's mouth. "Oh, Granny, what big teeth you have!"

Granny reached up and pulled off the wolf's head and smiled with teeth that were large indeed. Too large to be Granny's.

Because it wasn't Granny in the bed.

It was Horst.

I screamed and turned to run, but Horst snatched me by the cloak. I twisted and yanked to get free, but his grip was like iron. I reached up and undid the clasp of my cloak. It sent me pitching forward, but I caught myself in time and burst through the door.

"Goldie, run! It's Horst! Run!" I tripped over a tree root and tumbled to the ground.

"Red!" Goldie cried, pointing behind me. Horst came slowly toward me, my cloak still clutched in his fist. I tried to stand, but gasped with pain and faltered. I'd twisted my ankle.

A cold, hard hand wrapped around my arm and lifted me off the ground.

"Why are you afraid, little Red?" Horst said. "I only want to help."

I struggled to free myself. I kicked Horst as hard as I could and screamed as sharp pangs shot up my leg, but Horst did not let go. He didn't even wince.

"What did you do to Granny?" I demanded.

Horst smiled. It split across his withered face, sinister and grotesque. "You'll never see your granny again, not unless you give me the wolf."

"I won't!" I shouted, and yanked harder, straining my wrist.

"I must have a heart, Red. If you don't give me the wolf, then I'll have to find another heart." Horst brandished his long knife. "One I already have in my grasp."

Wolf growled, and bounded out of the trees. He attacked Horst, clamping his jaws around his neck.

"Wolf, no!" I shouted. Horst released me and heaved Wolf off of him. There was no blood where Wolf had bitten him, only teeth and claw marks, like gouges in clay. Wolf came at Horst again, growling, biting, and clawing, to no avail.

Horst's knife glinted silver as it slashed through the air. Wolf yelped and fell to the ground. I screamed and stumbled toward him, but Horst grabbed me by my hair.

Goldie attacked Horst, pummeling him with her tiny fists. "Stop it! Let her go, you mean man!"

Horst gave Goldie a small shove, and she fell.

"Goldie, run!" I shouted. "Get away as fast as you can!"

She shook her head. "I can't leave you! You'll die!"

Horst pulled my hair tighter. He pressed his knife to my throat. "Better run, little girl, before you meet the same fate as your friend."

Goldie kept shaking her head, tears running down her face.

I knew she wouldn't leave just to save herself. She was too kind, too loyal. But it was me Horst wanted. Me and Wolf. I couldn't allow Goldie to get hurt because of me.

"Goldie, I need you to get help. Run as fast as you can. Shout for help as loud as you can!"

Goldie wiped her tears. She stood up and ran through the trees, wailing for help.

I struggled once more to free myself, flinching at the cold blade against my skin.

"It looks as though your wolf friend won't be able to run from me any longer."

Wolf lay injured and helpless on the ground. He whined a little and struggled to get up, but fell back down.

And I had nothing to protect him. No path. No cloak. I was just a little girl. Just Red.

Red.

The tree nymphs rushed above me in the branches, whispering, clicking, sprinkling memories, and I remembered.

My name was supposed to be powerful. It was

supposed to be full of magic, like the red wine, the roses, and rubies. But it wasn't just my name. It was myself. *I* was full of magic. Granny said so. She said I was born with magic, and I heard her words now.

Red, don't be afraid.

Don't be afraid of what? A wolf? A huntsman? Death? Or was I only afraid of myself? My own destiny. My own magic, big and messy and—yes, sometimes it made fire and warts and roses out the nose, but that didn't mean it was *evil*. That didn't mean I couldn't be good.

I'd seen magic cause so many problems. Horrible curses, heartache, death. But I'd also seen it charm, delight, and heal. Inside of me, there was magic. I could feel it boiling to the surface, burning like rivers of fire in my veins. I had tried so hard to shove it down, to make it go away, but now it could not be contained.

I threw myself at Horst, releasing fiery magic so strong that it knocked him off his feet and sent him crashing into a tree. The tree gave a sickening crack. Horst was not hurt, only surprised. His eyes widened, and I saw the faintest flicker of fear in them, but then he steeled himself. He gnashed his teeth and rushed at me, roaring with beastly rage.

I stood my ground in front of Wolf. My heart pounded. It seemed to echo a spell, one that was all my own.

> *I am fearless.*
> *I am magic.*
> *I am Red.*

Horst raised his knife for one final attack to end it all. He cried out, and the blade came down, down, down, its sharp point hurtling toward my drumming, magic heart.

But the knife stopped just inches from my chest. Horst struggled, grunting with effort as he pressed it toward me, but some force pushed him back. I could feel the power emanating from me, springing from every part of me like branches growing out of a tree, like rays shooting from the sun. Horst grimaced. A crack formed in his hand. He trembled, pushing harder, until the crack spread up his arm and spiderwebbed over his knuckles. His skin turned a sickly gray, and more cracks crawled up his neck and face.

Horst's eyes grew panicked. All the fear he'd kept so carefully hidden now flooded to the surface. He emitted a deep groan, like a cave about to collapse. He dropped his knife and reached a hand out toward me in desperation until his fingers stiffened and crumbled like chalk. He fell to one knee, and his leg was crushed beneath the weight. The muscles in his neck tightened. His eyes turned dusty gray and hollow. Horst stretched his jaw in a silent scream as his whole body became solid stone.

A flurry of nymphs rushed down from the trees and swarmed around him then, whispering and clicking hungrily, drinking in the old huntsman's centuries of memories. They flew around him, faster and faster, building up a powerful cyclone, until the stone huntsman cracked in two, then disintegrated into a pile of dust.

As the power ebbed from me, my limbs grew cold.

The Woods grew utterly still and silent. I felt I was in a place I had never been before. The world felt different—or perhaps it was me who was different.

Wolf whimpered beneath me, pulling me from my trance. I fell to the ground and wrapped my arms around his neck. He was bleeding, but I couldn't tell how many wounds he had or how deep they were. My cloak lay on the ground beside him. I wrapped it around his body, pressing it into his wounds. Wolf whimpered and placed a paw on my knee.

Monster, he said. *Gone.*

"Yes," I said. "The monster is gone. You're safe now." I propped his head in my lap, and he seemed to relax.

A wind rushed through the trees, scattering the pile of dust that had been Horst the huntsman. Not dead. Just gone. Erased. No more. The magic he had sought so desperately to stop death had also stopped his life.

CHAPTER TWENTY-SIX

The Fate of Granny

I don't know how long Wolf and I remained alone in The Woods, whether it was minutes or hours, but eventually someone came for us.

"Red!" came a voice. Wolf sat up, his hackles raised and his ears pricked.

"It's all right." I tried to calm him. "It's just Goldie."

But she wasn't alone. Someone else was with her, and the presence spooked Wolf. He growled low, feeling threatened. "Don't be afraid," I said. "No one will hurt you."

"There she is! She's there with the wolf!" Goldie said. The person following Goldie started to run.

"Red?" It was a familiar voice, deep, edged with worry.

"Papa?"

I recognized his tall, strong frame. He carried an ax over his shoulder. Wolf bolted upright and growled, louder this time. Papa came after him with his ax. "Get away from her! Get!"

"No, don't!" I shouted. Wolf did not attack. He whimpered in fear and stumbled back. Papa stomped forward, brandishing his ax. Wolf turned and limped away through the trees.

"Wolf, wait!" I called. I stood and tried to go after him, but pain lanced up my leg. I had forgotten about my ankle. I grew dizzy. The earth seemed to tilt beneath me, and I fell.

"Red." Papa bent down and scooped me up in his arms. I pressed my head against his shoulder, comforted by his familiar smell of wood and wool. "Let's get you home."

"Wolf," I mumbled. "He's hurt."

"The wolf can't hurt you anymore," he said.

"No." I tried to explain, but I couldn't form the words. I could barely think, I was so tired. Papa carried me through The Woods, away from Wolf and toward home.

❧

The house was warm, but I felt cold inside. Papa sat me in a chair by the fire, and Mama was fussing all over me.

"What happened?" she asked. "Where are you hurt? Where did all this blood come from?" Mama brought a warm wet cloth and dabbed at my face. The cloth turned dark crimson.

"Wolf," I muttered. I needed to go to him, make sure he was all right.

"A wolf!" Mama exclaimed. "I told you she shouldn't be roaming alone through The Woods!"

"The huntsman," I started to explain.

"What about the huntsman? Did he kill the wolf?"

"He *tried* to kill the wolf," said Goldie. "He tried to kill Red, too, and me, too! He wanted our Magic Hearts!"

"What?" Mama looked back and forth between Goldie and me, completely befuddled. "Red, what is she talking about?"

"Wolf . . . the huntsman . . . ," I tried to explain, but I was interrupted by a goat.

Maa-a-a-aaa!

"Milk?" I said.

"Blasted goat," said Papa. "I don't know why she insists on keeping it indoors."

"She's a good guard goat!" said a voice, weak and hoarse but familiar. "Saved me from a terrible monster!"

My breath caught. My heart stopped. The voice was like a spell. It lifted me off the chair and pulled me over to Mama and Papa's room. Milk the guard goat was tethered to the bedpost, and in the bed was Granny. She was thin and pale. She was coughing into a handkerchief, and it sounded terrible, but she was alive. Granny was *alive*!

"Red, is that you? It's about time! I told your mama and papa you'd be just fine, but they got in such a tizzy it gave me a headache!"

My eyes blurred. A lump formed in my throat, and it

grew until I couldn't breathe, and something had to give. Tears burst from me like water from a broken dam.

"Good grief, child, what is the matter with you?"

"I . . . I thought you were dead!"

"Dead? What made you think I was dead?"

"Because you said you were dying."

"Well, of course I'm dying. Everybody dies. It's the most natural thing in the world."

"I know!" I laughed a little, and then I cried harder. I couldn't stop. There was just so much inside me, an endless well of feeling that I'd shoved down deep, wrapped up tight. Now it was bursting forth all at once, and it made me dizzy. My legs gave out beneath me. Papa picked me up in his arms and held me to his chest.

"Good grief," Granny repeated.

Papa carried me to the bed and laid me down gently next to Granny. Mama took off my shoes and stockings. "Her ankle is swollen," she said, and the reminder brought back the throbbing pain. She wrapped cool cloths around it, then tucked me beneath the blankets.

"Granny," I said.

"I'm right here, child," she said softly, and placed her hand in mine. I squeezed hard. It was old and wrinkled, but warm and alive.

"Don't die," I said.

"I won't if you won't," she said.

"Am I dying?" I asked. It felt as though I could be.

"No," said Granny. "You're living. We're all living. Now close your eyes, child. Sleep."

I believe she put a sleeping spell on me, because I closed my eyes and didn't wake for two days. I dreamt of Wolf wandering through The Woods, wounded and alone. I heard him howling, high and lonesome. I needed to find him, but I couldn't open my eyes.

When I finally woke, the house was quiet. Granny was sleeping beside me. It must have been early morning, the perfect opportunity for me to slip out of the house and into The Woods to find Wolf. I slid out of bed and gasped at the pain in my ankle. The swelling had gone down, but it was still tender. I hobbled toward the door.

Maaaaaa! bleated Milk. She was chewing on some grass at the foot of the bed.

"Hush!" I said. "Do you want to wake the whole house?"

Maaaaaa! Milk repeated, and Mama came rushing into the room.

"Tattletale," I said.

"Red, what are you doing?" Mama took me by the arm and led me back to bed. "You're not fit to walk!"

"I have to find Wolf," I said. "He needs help."

"What are you talking about? Are you fevered?" She felt my forehead. I was not fevered, but the more I tried to explain about Wolf and his needing my help, the more Mama thought I was addled and needed more rest.

"A wolf has other wolves to take care of him," said Mama. "But you're a human, and humans need rest."

Mama kept me in bed for a full week, and whenever I tried to escape, Milk the guard goat ratted me out. Goldie tried to visit every day, sometimes twice a day, but Mama would not allow her in until I was fully rested and my ankle was healed. When she was satisfied with my recovery, Mama allowed a short visit. Goldie marched in carrying a clay pot. She held it out to me, beaming, and I noticed that she had several red welts on her face and arms.

"Guess what?" She shoved the pot into my lap and I opened it up. It was honey.

"I can charm bees now!" She scratched at a welt on her cheek. "Almost. A few didn't take to my charming so much, but that doesn't matter, because guess what? I found something even better than honey. Mummy! My mummy came to find me! And I must have found some kind of magic, because she loves me, Red! She says she loves me more than anything in the entire world and that I should never run away ever again!"

"That's wonderful," I said.

"And guess what? Mummy says we can stay on The Mountain if I can find enough honey hives. I've found five, not including yours. You still need to put your name on it, though. We're going to sell the honey so I can stay here and be your best friend in the whole world forever as long as you live. So live a long time, okay?"

She wrapped her arms around my neck, and I got a mouthful of her curls, which made me sneeze.

"All right, Goldie girl," said Granny. "Back away before you smother my only grandchild with that hair of yours."

Goldie released me from her choke hold but leaned over and whispered in my ear, "Your granny's a little scary."

"I know," I said. "She *is* a witch, after all."

"I heard that," said Granny. "Now shoo. I want to talk to my grandchild alone."

Goldie scurried out of the room but then popped her head back in and said, "I'm glad you didn't die."

The room was very still and quiet after Goldie left. Granny hadn't spoken much since I'd been here. She slept a lot, and when she was awake, it seemed as though every movement and every word took a great deal of energy, so she said and did only the things that really mattered. It seemed a wise way to live, in any case.

"You went on quite an adventure," she said.

I nodded. "I met a dwarf," I said.

"At last! Was he terribly grumpy?"

"Worse than you in the morning."

"Hmph," said Granny. "Did you take him by the beard, then?"

"I did," I said. "His name is Borlen, and wouldn't you know it? He's the same dwarf you took by the beard all those years ago."

"You don't say!"

I nodded again. "He's two hundred and seventy-six years old! Did you know that dwarves can live for a thousand years?"

"I didn't!" said Granny.

"And do you know what they do with the gems they find? They eat them!"

"*Eat* them?" Granny seemed genuinely shocked, which was rare as rubies. "Maybe that's why they're so grouchy. He was a nasty little brute, that dwarf."

"Perhaps he wouldn't have been so nasty if you hadn't stolen all his gems."

"I didn't steal anything!" Granny said indignantly. "That little vagabond stole them from the prince!"

I shook my head. "The prince stole them from Borlen. He was only getting them back."

Granny's cheeks turned rosy. "Well. How was I supposed to know? He was a perfect little beast to me."

Speaking of beasts . . .

"Borlen showed me some Red Roses, ones that will make you live forever. They were made by a powerful enchantress."

"Oh?" Granny shifted uncomfortably.

"Granny, why did you turn Beauty into a beast?"

Granny scoffed. "I did nothing of the kind! She turned herself into a beast, the foolish brat."

"She's different now," I said. "Can't you change her back?"

"If she's really different, then she'll be able to change herself back," said Granny. "But she won't live forever if she becomes human."

"That's better than being a beast forever, I suppose."

"You suppose?"

I nodded.

"Well, that's a relief," said Granny. "I was afraid you were going to turn *me* into a beast to keep me from dying."

"I nearly did," I said. "And I almost brought you wine that would have made you young again."

"That sounds lovely. Why didn't you? Would the wine turn me into a troll?"

I shook my head. "The wine would have made you young, but it also would have taken away all your memories." And I told her about The Well Witch.

"Well, maybe that would be worth it," said Granny. "I should love to be young again."

"Even if you forgot me?" I asked.

"Maybe just for a day or two," she teased. "I was beautiful when I was young. Just gorgeous—"

"Everybody said so," I finished for her.

Granny smiled. She placed her hand on my cheek. "You see? I will always be here, Red."

"How?" I said with a trembling voice. I thought I had dried all my tears, but I could feel buckets more welling up in me.

"I never knew my own grandmother," she continued, "and my mother died long ago, but I feel them both with me, all the time, because I came from them. They are a part of me and they are a part of you, and so we all keep living through each other. No one really goes away for good."

I rubbed the edge of my cloak. It had been draped over me like a blanket. "In The Woods, my path kept fading, going in and out. I thought it meant that I had lost you, and it was like losing a part of myself."

Granny seemed confused. "What would my dying have to do with your path fading?"

"Because you made it. If you were gone, wouldn't the path go, too?"

"Silly girl, I never made that path. You did. You made it yourself when you weren't more than three years old. Don't you remember?"

That couldn't be right. "You made it for me after that bear attacked me. I remember wanting so badly to go see you, but I didn't want bears to get me. You told me they wouldn't get me if I wasn't afraid, and I said I wouldn't be afraid if I had something to protect me. And that's when my path appeared. . . ."

"Because you wanted it to," said Granny. "You made that path with your own magic, and it was some of the most wonderful magic I've ever seen."

I tried to take in what Granny was saying. The path was mine. I made it with my own magic, and it wasn't dangerous or awful. It guided. It protected. It was good.

"Then why did it disappear?" I asked. "I didn't want it to."

"Why did the princess want to live forever?" said Granny. "And Horst. Why did he so desperately need to keep living?"

"Because they didn't want to die?" I didn't see what this had to do with my path.

"But *why?*"

I thought for a moment. Why had I wanted to save Granny? Why would anyone try to stop death? I could think of dozens of reasons, but they all boiled down to one. "They were afraid," I said.

Granny nodded. "The Well Witch, the huntsman, the beast—they all sought magic that would make them live. But the magic was always born of fear. Nothing twists magic so much as fear, Red."

"And so my path disappeared because . . . I was afraid?"

"Magic does not cause trouble, Red. *Fear*. Fear is what makes the trouble. Why do you think I'm always telling you not to be afraid?"

"I *was* afraid," I said. "But I'm not anymore." I took my cloak and wrapped it around my shoulders. "I'm Red. Strong. Fearless."

"And just a tiny bit grumpy," said Granny.

"Just like you."

"Like me." Granny smiled, but there was something of sadness in it. "And will you be afraid when I die? Because I will, Red. Someday. Maybe soon, even."

I took a deep breath. "I will probably cry, and maybe even feel angry a little, or a lot."

"I should hope so," said Granny indignantly. "I'd be insulted if you didn't at least break a dish or two."

"Or set something on fire," I said.

"That's my girl."

"I will miss you every day," I said. "But I won't be afraid."

Granny smiled, and I thought I saw a small glisten in her eyes. "When you are missing me most, then you must grow something. Roses. I want you to grow me a whole forest of roses in my memory, so you'd better get practicing." Granny took a pot of dirt from the bedside and set it in my lap. "I'd like you to grow me a rose now, please. A red one. Booger blossoms are my favorite."

I laughed a little and took the pot. It sat heavily in my lap. I was still weak and tired from all that had happened. Even so, I could feel that familiar pulse of energy nestled in my belly. I settled my hands over the pot, and I let the magic rise to my fingertips and pour into the soil. Nothing happened at first, but I waited patiently until a small shoot sprouted from the soil and rose up and up. It thickened into a hearty stem and grew thorns and leaves and, finally, a bud at the top that swelled and split, revealing deep red petals that opened and curled into a perfect rose.

Granny sighed. "Oh, well. I would have preferred booger blossoms, but this will do."

I gaped at the rose I had grown with my own magic. Nothing had caught fire. Nothing had broken or exploded. It was a perfect red rose.

Granny leaned over and kissed my forehead, and a single tear spilled onto my face and ran down my cheek. "Rest, child. I'll still be here when you wake."

I closed my eyes and held tight to Granny, feeling her heart beat with mine, two hearts alive and full of magic.

EPILOGUE

On and On and On

In autumn, I walked through The Woods on my path. It was as strong as ever, clear and true and never flickering, because I wasn't afraid. I was strong. I was magic. I was Red. I climbed up The Mountain and stood on the highest peak. Across from me, there was a rocky ledge and a cave that served as a den to a newly formed wolf pack. Wolf had not come to me since that day in The Woods. At first, I called and searched for him. I worried that something bad had happened. What if some other huntsman had caught him or he'd gotten into a fight with some beast of The Woods? But then I heard him howling.

Come! he called, and my heart thrilled at the sound and invitation, until I realized it was not for me. Another wolf howled in response, their voices twining together in that lovely, longing song.

Come!

I could see Wolf now, just outside his den. Another wolf stood by his side, a gray female with white markings on her chest and paws, and behind them were three pups, fluffy and playful. Two gray and one black with just a tuft of white on his chest. Wolf had found a mate, and now he had a new pack. I was happy for him, but I could not repress the ache in my heart—the feeling that I'd lost a friend. That was okay, though. Granny says it's good to feel sadness in times of loss, because it means we have loved. It means we're truly alive.

Wolf stared back at me across the cliffs. I still felt that thread of connection between us, pulsing and tugging ever so slightly. The bond we shared would never go away, but he didn't need me anymore. He wasn't my pet. I was not his keeper. He was wild and powerful, and he would run with other wolves now. Just as I would run with humans.

"Red!" I could hear Goldie calling to me from below. I couldn't believe she'd followed me all the way up here. "Red! Come down, I have a surprise for you!"

I looked at the wolf pack one last time. Wolf dipped his head, acknowledging me, then turned his attention back to his pack. He picked up one of the cubs by the scruff while the others pounced on his back.

I climbed down from the top of The Mountain to Goldie. "What is it?" I asked.

"Come on!" said Goldie. "Wait till you see!" She took off at a run, and I ran after her. Her golden curls bounced wildly, and my red cloak billowed out behind me like wings. We danced through The Woods. We leapt over rocks and fallen trees, hurtled down a hillside to the stream where we first met Borlen, then splashed through the water. We ran and ran until I was nearly out of breath. Finally Goldie slowed. "Shhhhh," she said. "Listen." I heard a familiar hum. Bees darted around me, resting on my cloak, multiplying as we walked toward an old tree stump swarming with bees.

"Goldie, you found another honey hive!"

"And this one isn't owned by a bear!" she said.

I walked to the hive and dipped my hand inside. I pulled out a good chunk of honeycomb, dripping with golden honey.

Goldie licked her lips. "I think I see how it's done now. Let me try." She tried to approach the hive, but the bees immediately began to sting her. "Oh! Ouch! Vicious little beasts!" she cried as she swatted them away.

Some things never change.

Speaking of beasts, I had been thinking about Beast in the enchanted castle. I wanted to go back and see if she was still a beast, or if she was Beauty again. And I wanted to see the dwarves again, too. I wondered if Borlen would be just as grumpy as before, or if he might be happy to see me this time. Maybe he would take me someplace new and exciting, without any beard holding required.

Someday I would do all that, but for now I was happy to stay on The Mountain. Who knew how much time Granny had left? And Goldie needed me. I needed her, too. She was one of my dearest friends in all the world, along with Rump, and Granny, too. I'd found I couldn't have too many friends, and that saying goodbye to one didn't mean I couldn't say hello to another.

"Let's go home," I said. My path unfurled beneath my feet. Goldie stepped onto the path, too, and put her arm through mine. "Red, when I'm old and you're older and it's time for us to die, let's just die on the same day, okay?"

"Let's not think of dying," I said. "Let's just live every day together, for a long time. Shall we?"

"Oh, yes, that sounds glorious. I'll let you have as much honey as you want, every day, for our whole lives."

"I'll get the honey out of the hive for you." I took her hand. As Goldie had once said, red and gold have always gone well together.

A wind rushed in, and the tree nymphs swirled and whispered. I understood them now, ever since that day with Horst when I had let go of my fear. Fear doesn't only twist our magic, it also makes us forget. It made me forget who I was, the strength and the goodness I had inside me. But when I let go of my fear and faced what was before me, the memories came rushing back, like voices carried on the fingers of the wind. I saw myself in Granny's arms, my first breaths of life, and my naming. I watched my first steps into The Woods, where the trees towered like friendly giants and the animals spoke simple wisdom. They whispered Granny's spells and charms and potions, all her magic that would one day become mine.

I wouldn't waste a single second of life, not mine or Granny's or anyone's. I'd learn all I could—all about Granny, her magic, her mistakes, her enormous love. I'd grow things. I'd try not to set them on fire. I'd take in all of Granny that I could, all the magic, the stories, the laughter, all the Rose of her, and the Red. That way, when she did die, I'd still have everything she was inside of me. She'd stay alive in me, and after I was gone, I'd stay alive through others, and we'd never really go away. We'd just all grow together, like a forest, like the world, changing seasons and living on and on and on.

THE END

AUTHOR'S NOTE

When I was five or six, my grandmother sat my siblings and me on the couch in her formal living room and told us she had cancer. "I could die," she said, "so I really want you to appreciate me while you have the chance." I couldn't fully process what she was saying. Death was still a very abstract idea to me. All I knew was that it was a big deal.

Decades later, I look back at that experience as a prime example of my grandmother's flair for drama. My grandmother did not die of cancer. She went on to live another twenty-five years, and I came to know and appreciate her very well. In her last years of life, I had the privilege of going to her home once a week and recording her life stories. She was an extremely interesting person, a singer and actress, and very beautiful. She loved to show everyone old photographs of herself in costumes and ball gowns. "Wasn't I *gorgeous!*" she would say. Her life had a fairy-tale quality that drew me in. There was adventure and danger, tragedy and beauty, and even a bit of the supernatural.

When I started writing *Red,* my grandmother was mostly bedridden. She knew what I was writing and she knew that the character of Red's granny would be based on her. "Will I be on the cover?" she asked.

"Probably not."

"Well, why not? I'm a main character, aren't I?" (Far be it from my grandmother to play a supporting role!)

She continued to pester me, asking me about my progress and when she'd get to read it. I kept putting her off, said it was coming, but the truth was that I was struggling. Though I had a set of characters I found amusing, I couldn't quite find the main thread of the story—and in the midst of this struggle, my grandmother passed away. Her death somehow awoke me. It pulled everything into focus. I realized that the thing Red loved more than anything in the world was her granny, and the worst thing that could ever happen would be for Granny to die.

Death is a difficult subject. Whether it happens early or late in life—by natural causes, illness, or accident—its sting is still felt by the survivors. Everyone has a different reaction to it, and everyone has a different idea of what it means. This story was my way of understanding what it means to me. I miss my grandmother, but her life and death have made me feel the essence of something bigger than myself, a connection to everyone and everything. Though my grandmother never read this story, I could not have written it without her. Every day I still feel her beauty, hilarity, and love, because it's all part of me.

ACKNOWLEDGMENTS

Many thanks to my editor, Katherine Harrison. We've grown together over these past three books, and you've become an integral part of my creative process. Thanks to my agent, Michelle Andelman, always the steady voice of reason. Your enthusiasm, expertise, and support have been a lifeline in my early career.

Thanks to Janet Wygal, Artie Bennett, and the entire editorial team. You guys are like the friends that let me know when I have spinach in my teeth. I'm a mess without you!

To my trusty friends and beta readers—Krista Van Dolzer, Peggy Eddleman, Jenilyn Tolley, and Janet Leftley—thank you for reading rough versions that I'm sure were less than thrilling, but you've all given me such incredible insight and encouragement.

To my kids—Whitney, Ty, and Topher—I love how much pride you take in your mom's work. May it always be so, and may you all find such satisfaction in your own life adventures.

And to Scott, love of my life, best friend in the world, each book I write has a bit of you sprinkled throughout. They're usually the best parts.

Åll the tales say that Snow White
was a perfect little princess.
They say the seven dwarves were
sneezy and dopey and grumpy.
But did anyone ever ask the dwarves for
their side of the story?

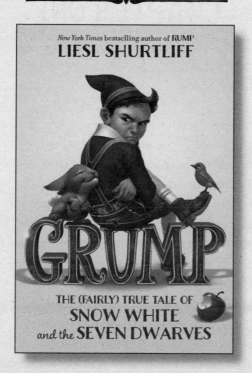

New York Times bestselling author of RUMP
LIESL SHURTLIFF

GRUMP

THE (FAIRLY) TRUE TALE OF
SNOW WHITE
and the SEVEN DWARVES

READ ON FOR A SNEAK PEEK!

CHAPTER ONE

Odd Little Dwarfling

I was born just feet from the surface of the earth, completely unheard of for a dwarf, but it couldn't be helped. Most dwarves are born deep underground, at least a mile below The Surface, preferably in a cavern filled with crystals and gems: diamonds for strength, emeralds for wisdom, and sapphires for truth.

Mothers and fathers try to feed their dwarflings as many healthy powerful gems as they can within a few hours of birth, to give them the best chance in life. But I was fed none.

My parents had been traveling downward the day I was born. Mother could feel me turning hard inside her belly, a sign that the time was drawing near. She wanted the very best for me. She wanted to be as deep in the earth as possible, in the birthing caverns, with their rich deposits of nutritious crystals and gems. But as my parents traveled downward, before they had even descended below the main caverns, there was a sudden collapse in one of the tunnels. The rocks nearly crushed my mother, and me with her. My father was able to get us out of the way just in time.

Unfortunately, the collapse had blocked the tunnel, so we had to go up to find another way down. The strain of the climb was too much for my poor mother.

"Rubald!" she cried, clutching her belly. "It's time!"

And there was no time to waste. A dwarfling can stay inside its mother's belly for a solid decade or more, but when we're ready to come out, we come fast.

And so I was born in a cavern mere feet below the earth's surface, where roots dangled from the ceiling, water trickled down the walls, and the only available food was a salty gruel called *strolg*, made out of common rocks and minerals. Mother was devastated.

"My poor little dwarfling!" she cooed as she spooned the strolg into my mouth, then fed me a few pebbles to satisfy my need to bite and crunch. "What kind of life will he have, Rubald?"

"A fine life, Rumelda," said my father, ever the optimist. "A happy life."

"And what will we call him?"

My parents both looked at their surroundings. Dwarves were usually named with some regard to the gems and crystals within the cavern in which they were born, but there were no diamonds or sapphires in that cavern. Not even quartz or marble. Just plain rocks and roots.

Father brushed his hands over the rough walls, studying the layers of dirt and minerals. "Borlen," he said with wonder.

Borlen was a mineral found only near The Surface. It was not so common in our colony but useful when it could be found. It was too bitter to eat, but potters liked it because it made their clay more malleable without weakening it. Borlen could also serve as a warning. A mining crew knew by the sight of it that they were digging dangerously close to The Surface. Most dwarves would rather not find any.

"We'll call him Borlen," said Father.

"You don't think that name will make him seem a bit . . . odd?" Mother asked.

"No, it's special," said Father. "He'll be one of a kind, our dwarfling. We'll get him deep into the earth as soon as possible and feed him all the best crystals and gems. But wait!" My father pulled something from his pocket and held it out to my mother. "I almost forgot. I've been saving this from the moment I knew we had a dwarfling on the way."

Mother gasped. "A ruby!"

Rubies were rare and particularly powerful gems. They could ward off evil, enhance powers, and even lengthen lives. Emegert of Tunnel 588 was said to have found a large deposit of rubies, and he lived for ten thousand years. Two thousand years was considered a good long life for a dwarf.

Mother took the ruby from my father and dropped it onto my tongue. I crunched on the gem, gave a little belch, and fell asleep.

The very next day, my parents tried to move me to deeper caverns, but as soon as they started to carry me downward, I began to cry. The deeper we went, the louder I wailed, until my eyes leaked tears of dust, a sign of deep distress and discomfort from any dwarf.

"Oh dear," said Mother. "Rubald, I think our dwarfling is afraid of depths!"

"Nonsense," said Father. "He only needs to adjust."

But I did not adjust. I cried for hours on end. My parents tried everything to console me. They fed me amber, amethysts, and blue-laced agate. They bathed me in crushed rose quartz and hung peridot above my cradle, all to no avail. And so, distraught from my endless wails, and desperate to try anything, my parents took me back to the cavern near The Surface where I was born.

I stopped crying.

"Oh dear," said Mother.

"How odd," said Father.

And after that, my parents were obliged to make my unfortunate birthing cavern our home, hoping my fear of depths would subside eventually. But it didn't. It only got worse.

❧

For years, my parents worked to get me used to depths. Father tried to lead me a little deeper each day, luring me with my favorite gems and the different sites and wonders of the colony—the lava rivers, the blue springs, the dragon hatchery, the potters and glass blowers and gold-smiths. But no matter how interesting the surroundings, no matter how many sapphires and rubies he offered, my depth symptoms would always overpower me. I'd start to get dizzy, then I'd feel like I was shrinking and shriveling, and we'd have to go back home.

It was shameful enough that I was afraid of depths, but that wasn't the worst of it. As much as I hated going downward, I was equally drawn to going upward. My first word was "up," much to my parent's chagrin, and as soon as I understood that there was an actual world above us, I wanted to know everything about it. I pestered my parents with questions. What did The Surface look like? How was it different from our caves? Did any dwarves live up there? Why didn't *we* live up there? Could we go there?

My parents knew next to nothing about The Surface. Neither of them had seen it, nor had any desire to. Mother usually sidestepped my questions or changed the subject, but Father indulged my curiosity. He took me to the colony's record room—a vast cavern filled with many millennia of our history and collective knowledge engraved on stone tablets and slates. Normally, I wouldn't have tolerated the depths of the cavern, but my thirst for information overcame my fear. I scoured the records for any facts I could find about The Surface. I learned it was a big, open place with an endless blue ceiling called the *sky*, and a big golden ball suspended in the sky called the *sun*. There were things that grew on The Surface that didn't grow underground. Things called *trees* and *flowers* and *bushes*. There were strange beasts that roamed The Surface—*horses*, *bears*, and *wolves*. But the most fascinating of all were the *humans*.

According to the records, humans were dwarflike creatures, but not really dwarves at all. They could grow three times the height of a dwarf but no wider. They were born without teeth, and they lived no more than a single century. They couldn't eat gems but, instead, wore them around their necks, on their fingers and wrists, and sometimes even on their heads. I imagined a giant, skinny dwarf with no teeth, wearing my dinner as a hat. I laughed at the thought. I definitely had to see that spectacle!

In a magical kingdom where your name
is your destiny, twelve-year-old Rump is the
butt of everyone's joke, until an old spinning
wheel changes everything. . . .

READ ON FOR A SNEAK PEEK!

CHAPTER ONE

Your Name Is Your Destiny

My mother named me after a cow's rear end. It's the favorite village joke, and probably the only one, but it's not really true. At least I don't think it's true, and neither does Gran. Really, my mother had another name for me, a wonderful name, but no one ever heard it. They only heard the first part. The worst part.

Mother had been very ill when I was born. Gran said she was fevered and coughing and I came before I was supposed to. Still, my mother held me close and whispered my name in my ear. No one heard it but me.

"His name?" Gran asked. "Tell me his name."

"His name is Rump . . . *haaa-cough-cough-cough* . . ." Gran gave Mother something warm to drink and pried me from her arms.

"Tell me his name, Anna. All of it."

But Mother never did. She took a breath and then let out all the air and didn't take any more in. Ever.

Gran said that I cried then, but I never hear that in my imagination. All I hear is silence. Not a move or a breath. The fire doesn't crack and even the pixies are still.

Finally, Gran holds me up and says, "Rump. His name is Rump."

The next morning, the village bell chimed and gnomes ran all over The Mountain crying, "Rump! Rump! The new boy's name is Rump!"

My name couldn't be changed or taken back, because in The Kingdom your name isn't just what people call you. Your name is full of meaning and power. Your name is your destiny.

My destiny really stinks.

I stopped growing when I was eight and I was small to begin with. The midwife, Gertrude, says I'm small because I had only the milk of a weak goat instead of a strong mother, but I know that really it's because of my name. You can't grow all the way if you don't have a whole name.

I tried not to think about my destiny too much, but on my birthday I always did. On my twelfth birthday I thought of nothing else. I sat in the mine, swirling mud around in a pan, searching for gold. We needed gold, gold, gold, but all I saw was mud, mud, mud.

The pickaxes beat out a rhythm that rang all over The Mountain. It filled the air with thumps and bumps. In my head The Mountain was chanting, *Thump, thump, thump. Bump, bump, bump. Rump, Rump, Rump.* At least it was a good rhyme.

> *Thump, thump, thump*
> *Bump, bump, bump*
> *Rump, Rump, Rump*

"Butt! Hey, Butt!"

I groaned as Frederick and his brother Bruno approached with menacing grins on their faces. Frederick and Bruno were the miller's sons. They were close to my age, but so big, twice my size and ugly as trolls.

"Happy birthday, Butt! We have a present just for you." Frederick threw a clod of dirt at me. My stubby hands tried to block it, but it smashed right in my face and I gagged at the smell. The clod of dirt was not dirt.

"Now that's a gift worthy of your name!" said Bruno.

Other children howled with laughter.

"Leave him alone," said a girl named Red. She glared at Frederick and Bruno, holding her shovel over her shoulder like a weapon. The other children stopped laughing.

"Oh," said Frederick. "Do you love Butt?"

"That's not his name," growled Red.

"Then what is it? Why doesn't he tell us?"

"Rump!" I said without thinking. "My name is Rump!" They burst out laughing. I had done just what they wanted. "But that's not my real name!" I said desperately.

"It isn't?" asked Frederick.

"What do you think his real name is?" asked Bruno.

Frederick pretended to think very hard. "Something unusual. Something special . . . Cow Rump."

"Baby Rump," said Bruno.

"Rump Roast!"

Everyone laughed. Frederick and Bruno fell over each other, holding their stomachs while tears streamed down their faces. They rolled in the dirt and squealed like pigs.

Just for a moment I envied them. They looked like they were having such fun, rolling in the dirt and laughing. Why couldn't I do that? Why couldn't I join them?

Then I remembered why they were laughing.

Red swung her shovel down hard so it stuck in the ground right between the boys' heads. Frederick and Bruno stopped laughing. "Go away," she said.

Bruno swallowed, staring cross-eyed at the shovel that was just inches from his nose. Frederick stood and grinned at Red. "Sure. You two want to be alone." The brothers walked away, snorting and falling over each other.

I could feel Red looking at me, but I stared down at my pan. I picked out some of Frederick and Bruno's present. I did not want to look at Red.

"You'd better find some gold today, Rump," said Red.

I glared at her. "I know. I'm not *stupid*."

She raised her eyebrows. Some people did think I was stupid because of my name. And sometimes I thought they were probably right. Maybe if you have only half a name, you have only half a brain.

I kept my eyes on my pan of mud, hoping Red would go away, but she stood over me with her shovel, like she was inspecting me.

"The rations are tightening," said Red. "The king—"

"I *know*, Red."

Red glared at me. "Fine. Then good luck to you." She stomped off, and I felt worse than when Frederick and Bruno threw poop in my face.

Red wasn't my friend exactly, but she was the closest I had to a friend. She never made fun of me. Sometimes she stood up for me, and I understood why. Her name wasn't all that great, either. Just as people laugh at a name like *Rump*, they fear a name like *Red*. *Red* is not a name. It's a color, an *evil* color. What kind of destiny does that bring?

I swirled mud in my pan, searching for a glimmer. Our village lives off The Mountain's gold—what little there is to find. The royal tax collector gathers it and takes it to the king. King Barf. If King Barf is pleased with our gold, he sends us extra food for rations. If he's not pleased, we are extra hungry.

King Barf isn't actually named King Barf. His real name is King Bartholomew Archibald Reginald Fife, a fine, kingly name—a name with a great destiny, of course. But I don't care how handsome or powerful that name makes you. It's a mouthful. So for short I call him King Barf, though I'd never say it out loud.

A pixie flew in my face, a blur of pink hair and translucent wings. I held still as she landed on my arm and explored. I tried to gently shake her off, but she only fluttered her wings and continued her search. She was looking for gold, just like me.

Pixies are obsessed with gold. Once, they had been very helpful in the mines since they can sense large veins of gold from a mile away and deep in the earth. Whenever a swarm of pixies would hover around a particular spot of rock, the miners knew precisely where they should dig.

But there hasn't been much gold in The Mountain for many years. We find only small pebbles and specks. The pixies don't dance and chirp the way they used to. Now they're just pests, pesky thieves trying to steal what little gold we find. And they'll bite you to get it. Pixies are no bigger than a finger and they look sweet and delicate and harmless with their sparkly wings and colorful hair, but their bites hurt worse than bee stings and squirrel bites and poison ivy combined—and I've had them all.

The pixie on my arm finally decided I had no gold and flew away. I scooped more mud from the sluice and swirled it around in my pan. No gold. Only mud, mud, mud.

Thump, thump, thump
Bump, bump, bump
Rump, Rump, Rump

I didn't find any gold. We worked until the sun was low and a gnome came running through the mines shouting, "The day is done! The day is done!" in a voice so bright and cheery I had the urge to kick the gnome and send it flying down The Mountain. But I was relieved. Now I could go home, and maybe Gran had cooked a chicken. Maybe she would tell me a story that would help me stop thinking about my birth and name and destiny.

I set my tools aside and walked alone down The

Mountain and through The Village. Red walked alone too, a little ahead of me. The rest of the villagers traveled in clusters, some children together, others with their parents. Some carried leather purses full of gold. Those who found good amounts of gold got extra rations. If they found a great deal, they could keep some to trade in the markets. I had never found enough gold even for extra rations.

Pixies fluttered in front of my face and chirped in my ears, and I swatted at them. If only the pixies would show me a mound of gold in the earth, then maybe it wouldn't matter that I was small. If I found lots of gold, then maybe no one would laugh at me or make fun of my name. Gold would make me worth something.

You might think you know all about
giants and beanstalks
and that foolish boy who traded
his family's cow for some magic beans.
But you don't know JACK!

READ ON FOR A SNEAK PEEK!

> Jack was brisk and of a ready,
> lively wit, so that nobody or
> nothing could worst him.
>
> —Jack the Giant Killer

CHAPTER ONE

A Sprinkling of Dirt

When I was born, Papa named me after my great-great-great-great-great-great-GREAT-grandfather, who, legend had it, conquered nine giants and married the daughter of a duke. Mama said this was all hogwash. Firstly, there was no such thing as giants. Wouldn't we see such large creatures if they really existed? And secondly, we had no relation to any duke—if we did, we'd be rich and living on a grand estate. Instead, we were poor as dirt and lived in a tiny house on a small farm in a little village. Nothing great or giant about it.

But Papa wasn't concerned with the details. He

believed there was greatness in that name, and if he gave it to me, somehow the greatness would sink into my bones.

"We'll name him Jack," Papa said. "He'll be great."

"If you say so," said Mama. She was a practical woman and not particular with names. All she needed was a word to call me to supper, or deliver a scolding. I got my first scolding before my first supper, just after birth, for as soon as Papa pronounced my name, I sprang a sharp tooth, and bit my mother.

"Ouch!" Mama cried. "You naughty boy!" It was something she would call me more often than Jack.

Papa had the nerve to laugh. "Oh, Alice, he's just a baby. He doesn't know any better."

But Mama believed I *did* know better. To her, that bite was a little omen of what was to come, like a sprinkle before the downpour, a buzz before the sting, or the onset of an itch before you realize you're covered in poison ivy.

Maybe I was born to be great, but great at what?

At five months old, I learned to crawl. I was fast as a cockroach, Papa said. One minute I was by Mama's skirts, and the next I was in the pigsty, rolling around in the muck and slops. Mama said she had to bathe me twice a day just to keep me from turning into a real pig.

I learned to walk before my first year, and by my second I took to climbing. I climbed chairs and tables, the woodpile, trees. Once Mama found me on the roof, and snatched me up before I slid down the chimney into a blazing fire.

"Such a naughty boy," said Mama.

"He's just a boy," said Papa.

But I didn't want to be "just a boy." I wanted to be great.

At night, Papa would tell stories of Grandpa Jack: how he'd chop off giants' heads and steal all their treasure and rescue the innocents. I knew if I was going to be great, I'd have to go on a noble quest and conquer a giant—or nine—just like my seven-greats-grandpa Jack.

There was only one problem. I'd never seen a giant in all my twelve years.

It all happened once upon a time....

READ ALL THE *NEW YORK TIMES* BESTSELLING (FAIRLY) TRUE TALES!

"Lighthearted and inventive."
—Brandon Mull, #1 *New York Times* bestselling author of *Fablehaven*

"Liesl Shurtliff has the uncanny ability to make magical worlds feel utterly real." —Tim Federle, author of *Better Nate Than Ever*

"*Red* is the most wonder-filled fairy tale of them all!" —Chris Grabenstein, *New York Times* bestselling author of *Escape from Mr. Lemoncello's Library*

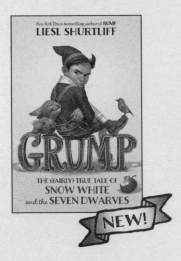

NEW!